KU-707-323

Millie Adams has always loved books. She considers herself a mix of Anne Shirley—loquacious, but charming, and willing to break a slate over a boy's head if need be—and Charlotte Doyle—a lady at heart, but with the spirit to become a mutineer should the occasion arise. Millie lives in a small house on the edge of the woods, which she finds allows her to escape in the way she loves best: in the pages of a book. She loves intense alpha heroes and the women who dare to go toe-to-toe with them. Or break a slate over their heads…

Also by Millie Adams

The Kings of California miniseries

The Scandal Behind the Italian's Wedding
Stealing the Promised Princess
Crowning His Innocent Assistant

Discover more at millsandboon.co.uk.

FALKIRK COMMUNITY TRUST

30124 02697337 2

2 4 MAR

THE ONLY KING TO CLAIM HER

MILLIE ADAMS

MILLS & BOON

All rights reserved including the right of reproduction
in whole or in part in any form. This edition is
published by arrangement with Harlequin Books S.A.

This is a work of fiction. Names, characters,
places, locations and incidents are purely fictional
and bear no relationship to any real life individuals,
living or dead, or to any actual places, business
establishments, locations, events or incidents.
Any resemblance is entirely coincidental.

This book is sold subject to the condition that it
shall not, by way of trade or otherwise, be lent, resold,
hired out or otherwise circulated without the prior consent
of the publisher in any form of binding or cover
other than that in which it is published and without a
similar condition including this condition being
imposed on the subsequent purchaser.

® and TM are trademarks owned and used by the
trademark owner and/or its licensee. Trademarks
marked with ® are registered with the United Kingdom
Patent Office and/or the Office for Harmonisation in the
Internal Market and in other countries.

First published in Great Britain 2021
by Mills & Boon, an imprint of HarperCollins*Publishers* Ltd,
1 London Bridge Street, London, SE1 9GF

www.harpercollins.co.uk

HarperCollins*Publishers*
1st Floor, Watermarque Building,
Ringsend Road, Dublin 4, Ireland

Large Print edition 2021

The Only King to Claim Her © 2021 Millie Adams

ISBN: 978-0-263-28918-3

12/21

FALKIRK COUNCIL LIBRARIES

MIX
Paper from
responsible sources
FSC C007454

This book is produced from independently certified
FSC™ paper to ensure responsible forest management.
For more information visit www.harpercollins.co.uk/green.

Printed and bound in the UK using 100% Renewable
Electricity at CPI Group (UK) Ltd, Croydon, CR0 4YY

For all who need strength
to tackle the next battle:
'There are far, far better things ahead
than any we leave behind.'
—C.S. Lewis

CHAPTER ONE

MAXIMUS KING LOOKED across the ballroom at Arianna Lopez, who up until tonight had been a disgraced starlet working her way back into the good graces of society. Optics were everything in this age of social media. Constant visibility.

Arianna had made the terrible mistake of being beautiful, rich, and seeming selfish. And so, had fallen out of favor with the clambering masses on the internet who saw her as a property belonging to them.

And rehabilitating image was his business. Tonight had been a sterling success. The charity event was sparkling, and perfect. And she now looked more Madonna than whore.

His job was done.

She was the same shallow, ridiculous creature she'd been when they'd met two weeks ago. But now the world had forgotten her tantrum about the roses she was given not being entirely white, and so it didn't matter what was in her heart.

Only what people saw.

Optics, after all, were everything.

With every aspect of a person's life available for public consumption nowadays, it had to be so.

Perhaps it was why he took such great, perverse delight in using optics as his cover.

For no one, not even his family, knew the truth about Maximus King.

He straightened his tie and turned, beginning to walk out of the room. He heard the click of high heels behind him.

He paused. He knew that it was Arianna; he had noted the sound her shoes made against the marble floor. No one ever took him off guard.

"Are you leaving?"

"Yes," he said.

"I thought that we might…leave together. After all, our working relationship was so satisfactory. I thought we might be able to… transition it." She put one delicate, manicured hand on his shoulder, and her touch left him cold.

But he smiled. That charming grin of the playboy that all the world took him to be. "Not tonight."

"Not tonight?" Her eyes widened. "I was under the impression you're up for it every night."

He gave her his best, most practiced grin. Nothing to see here, just a playboy. Not a care in the world. "There's already a woman waiting in my bed, sweetheart." He winked for good measure. "You have to book early."

He turned and continued to walk out of the ballroom. His car was there at the front of the hotel waiting for him. He scanned the street, a habit. Then got into the vehicle, maneuvering through the San Diego streets, making his way back to his glittering mansion in the hills. He had a spectacular view of the ocean from the front, and the protection of the mountains in the back.

Lots of windows.

With bulletproof glass.

Again, part of the facade. An appearance

of vulnerability, of openness. Without actually offering it.

He parked his car in front of the house and got out, using the fingerprint sensor to allow him entry into the home.

And the moment he stepped into the darkened room, he felt something was off.

He paused and reached into his suit jacket. He had a small gun there with a silencer. He always carried it.

As he walked deeper into the house, he heard nothing. Rather, he sensed a ripple of disturbance in the air. He had learned to listen to his gut. It was the difference between life and death. And he was still alive.

"I would quite rather you did not shoot me."

The voice coming from the darkness was feminine, accented and sweet.

"Who are you?" he asked.

He heard a rustle of movement, coming from inside the living room, and then he saw a figure, dressed in white, moving toward him. She stepped into a shaft of moonlight that filtered in from the windows that faced the sea. Small, with long blond hair and a round, pale face, he could not make her features out in the dim light.

"I am Princess Annick, formerly of the lower dungeon. Lately of the palace proper."

Something echoed inside of him.

"Annick," he repeated.

He knew the name Annick. *Princess* Annick.

"Who sent you?"

"*I* sent me," she said. "A perk, I suppose, of being free. And I am free." She made a small sound that might've been a laugh. "Peculiar, that. I am not accustomed to it."

"You're the Princess of Aillette, correct?" He knew.

He didn't need her to confirm. He'd taken an assignment there only a year ago. That meant he'd learned the history of the country and he would not forget it. He took his work seriously, and that meant he didn't go in and perform the task unless he was quite clear on what was being done.

As far as the US government was concerned, there was no Maximus King enlisted in their ranks. His work, and any trail that could be traced back to him, was so coded it would take a mastermind to track him down.

Granted, he had always known it was possible. Hence the bulletproof glass.

But he still could not quite figure out how this woman was here, now, and with full knowledge of both his lives.

"Oui," she said. "It is me."

"I have already done a service for your country, Annick. I'm not certain why you are here."

"Oh, it is in regard to that service, Mr. King."

"I don't do follow-up visits."

"Ah, but you see, you have created a problem."

"Removing dictators from power is the solution. Not the problem."

"What of the vacuum that is left behind?"

"Not my responsibility."

"Eh," she said. "Then what is?"

"Just as I said. I receive orders from military intelligence. I gather a team, or simply myself, depending on the situation. I carry out orders. I leave. I assume that the government sends a crew in after to handle the rest."

"Ha! Lip service at best," she said. "Three months of transitional assistance and then what? Gone. I am left with few resources, and little path to rule a country that still scarcely believes I am mentally well enough to rule. Though I believe I have been perfectly wonderful in the year since I have begun to rule."

"You claim to have few resources, and yet here you are."

"I am very sneaky," she said. "And that comes from many years of imprisonment and secret plotting for how I might make amends when I was released."

"Were you not complicit in the regime?"

"I was certainly *not*. As I said, I was primarily ensconced in the lower dungeon. I was trotted out as a figurehead on rare occasions. Proof of life and all. And I confess, if I have one weakness it is that I do care a bit for my life. I did not wish to be dead."

"A common wish," he said.

"Quite."

"So what is it you want, Annick? Other than to not be dead."

She looked up at him, and for a moment, he thought he saw her falter. For a moment, he saw vulnerability. "I would like for you to come back to Aillette with me."

"No."

"You have not even heard my proposition."

"I don't need to."

"You should hear my proposition, I think."

"You are perhaps overrating your proposition. I have so much here," he said, indicating the mansion that he did not care about at all. He was dead inside. And when you were dead inside, you did not fear death, not overmuch. But Annick did not need to know that. Annick only needed to know what the rest of the world knew about him. Though she did know a few things, which he found disturbing. She knew that he was responsible for the death of the dictator of Aillette.

Annick had joined his two lives together.

A problem.

But he was not in the business of dispatching small women.

It was only ever those who deserved it.

Only ever those who had committed great and terrible atrocities. He did not consider himself to be a good man, but he was a man looking for a way to balance the scales in the world.

To try and fix what he had not managed to fix all those many years ago.

And nothing would bring Stella back.

He remained, she was gone and it did not fix itself, no matter how many deserving people he took out of the world. But he considered it his payment.

A way to try and at least put some sort of balance out into the universe.

Annick looked at him and lifted a shoulder. "I require a small thing. I need you to return to my country with me. To act as my guard."

She had successfully silenced the brute.

She had done a decent amount of research into Maximus King before stealing away to San Diego to confront him. He was a fascinating character. She found she was not frightened of him, though she perhaps should be. But she was not easily frightened.

For her entire family had been lost to her as

a child, and she had been trotted in and out of the dungeon ever since. Educated, made to appear somewhat civilized.

They thought she had been made loyal.

But she had been lying, for all her life, out of a sense of self-preservation. And now she finally had a chance to make up for it all. Now she had a chance to finally make a difference. To make the years of farce worthwhile.

She just had to convince this playboy, who she was given to believe was a secret assassin, to become her protector.

She needed a man by her side. This was the problem.

Annick was a realist. You could not live ten years as a prisoner without being a realist. The world was harsh. And nobody cared if you were a child. Nobody cared when there was power to be had.

Annick had been forced to play the part of silent figurehead to a country that she loved, to stand beside men who made her burn with hatred and smile. So that for all the world to see, Aillette was a functioning government.

It was not.

Her people were badly treated.

Reform. Revolution.

Those had been the rallying cries of the men who had stormed the palace and destroyed her family.

It had been none of those things.

And now that she was back in power she would see that her people were never harmed again. She needed his protection. For her people, not so much for her.

Dangerous men did not scare her.

She had made a bargain with herself when dealing with such men for many years now. Making a bargain with a man such as this bothered her not at all.

"You wish me to return to Aillette with you?"

"I more than wish it. I command it."

"Or?"

"I will think nothing of exposing your identity."

"You see, in order for that to concern me," he said, his voice hard, "I would have to care a great deal more for my life than I do."

He was bluffing. At least, she was counting on this being a bluff. If it was not, then she might have a little trouble.

But he was. Surely.

This was the part she'd known she must steel herself for. Threats made her stomach shake. She did not wish to issue them. But she would do what she must.

"Your sister Violet? Who is a Princess, I believe, in Monte Blanco. What would become of her and her country, of her husband, if the world found out that her brother was an assassin?"

His eyes went sharp. Good. "You are playing a dangerous game, Annick."

"Life is a dangerous game, is it not? And what of Minerva. Your sweet sister and her lovely children. Her husband. Your mother and father. What of them? If your identity was known, then their safety would be at risk."

"You dare threaten my family?"

"They are not threats." She shook her head. "I am merely presenting you with a piece of reality. It is not a threat—it is just true."

"The end result of your truth is that innocent people, innocent children, may die."

"Innocent people, innocent children, have died in my country already," she said. "And if I cannot successfully wrest control here, do I not risk another revolution? An invasion from my neighbors? Yes, I think I do. I *know* I do. I am not open to such risk-taking."

"And yet you have taken a risk coming here." He reached into his pocket and took a device out, and with a flick of his wrist, the lights came on.

She blinked against the invasive brightness. She had seen pictures of him, but they did not do him justice. He was a very large man, broad, with dark brown hair.

His face was handsome. Uncommonly so. She had never seen a man with quite such a competent scaffolding. A strange thing, human beauty. For it was just an arrangement of features and skin placed over bone in a particular fashion.

Yet his was quite striking.

And it made a sensation stir low in her belly. One that was foreign to her. It reminded her a great deal of fear, but it was not that. She was not afraid. Then she noticed that in one of his hands he still held the gun. The light revealed the weapon she had known was there all along.

Though she had the sense just then that the true weapon was the man himself.

"Please do not shoot me."

"I've no desire to shoot you. Therefore, to please us both—you and your desire to not be dead, me and my desire to not shoot a woman—I suggest you leave, and forget this conversation ever occurred."

"I cannot. I *cannot*, because it is what must be done for my people. I have been over many solutions. *Many.* Are you a man who desires power? As my guard, as my... my right-hand man, you would be very powerful."

"No. If I desired power, don't you think I would have filled one of the vacant positions I left behind already?"

"And that is a strange thing," she said. "Because most men do desire power, do they not?"

"I suppose, to an extent. But then, I often wonder if such men have ever been up close to it."

"Yes, a good observation, I think. For

power does not entice me, personally. It is only that I must take it, as is my responsibility. My birthright. All my family are dead."

"I'm sorry. But you have presented a scenario wherein *my* family might all be dead."

"It is not what I want, Maximus King. I hope you understand. What I want is for the safety of my country to be secured. What I want is for you to help steady the situation that you have created."

"Again, the situation was not mine."

"Whose?"

"Your neighbors to the east, in Lackland. I believe they thought it better to depose the despot in power for their own reasons."

"Yes, for reasons likely of taking over. Which I do not want either. So, you can see the situation I find myself in. I need money. Would you not like to have this power?"

"As I said, I am not overly enamored of power."

"Then why do you do it? Why do you do this…this insipid job you pretend to do? What is it, repairing the reputations of Hollywood stars? And you kill people for money."

"I carry out missions assigned to me. And

often that results in the deaths of men who would kill countless others. Countless innocents."

"You and the government then decide who is good and who is bad? What is that, if not an exercise in power? Playing God. Playing God with public opinion, playing God with life. Do not tell me you don't wish for power. I am not stupid, me."

She wondered, for a moment, if she had gone too far. He did not frighten her, not really. But she was very aware of the fact that if she pushed him too far, she would not get what she wanted, and that did frighten her. For she had no other plan. No other idea for how she might bail her country out of the disaster it found itself in.

"What other enticements have you to offer?"

She fortified herself with a breath. For she had been prepared for this moment. "Me. My body."

He looked her up and down. "Please do not take this the wrong way, but I have no need."

She narrowed her eyes, feeling insulted. "What does that mean?"

"I do not need to take a woman in trade for anything. If I want a woman, I simply have her."

"Not me."

"And that is supposed to be of particular enticement to me?"

She lifted a shoulder. "*No* man has had me. A shock, I would think, given that I have been kept prisoner for so long. But I think it was quite a game, right? To keep me untouched. For future leverage. Virginity is valuable."

His gaze flickered dispassionately over her again. "Is it? Here it is quite disposable. Something to throw away at the earliest of conveniences."

"Well, not for me. For every indignity I have suffered, for all that has been taken, not that. But I will give it to you."

"I don't have a need of your virginity, Princess. I didn't even need my own. It's been gone for twenty years and I haven't missed it."

"Money, then. What I have is a land rich with minerals. Gold and oil. Untapped. The dictators, they were not so smart, I think.

But I learned a great many things, because I had nothing but time. So, I read. And what I discovered is that there is much unexplored in my country. But I need the investment to see it done. And I need to live. I need to keep living, or none of it matters. And for that I need you."

"You think you can buy me?"

"You are bought. Repeatedly. Do not pretend to be a man of great principle now. If you are a man of great principle, then you would perform your task for free, but you do not."

"No one works for free."

"Yes, see? That is what I'm saying. No one works for free, and I do not expect you to. You protect me, and I will reward you in the end. Consider it a new mission, but this time you fix what it is you broke."

"You believe you need a guard? That you are in danger? And for how long do you foresee needing this?"

"I am to be crowned Queen soon, and I think…some time. It has been held off by the council, my coronation, to see if I am fit after my time as prisoner. And I worry the neighboring countries…lie in wait. It will take time."

"How much time?" he asked, impatient now.

"My neighbors in Lackland are a threat to me," she said. "I have intelligence that says they will overthrow me."

"From where?"

"Your government," she said, waving a hand. "Such a help they were, ridding us of dictator extraordinaire Pierre Doucet, and such aid was given! For all of three months and now I am threatened and on my own. So you see, I get insurance of my own. Protection of my own. And it is fair I confiscate one of their resources to do it."

"The resource being me?"

"Oui."

"You're trying to play the victim here, Annick, and yet you lead with a threat to my family?"

"You lead with a gun. So, seems fair."

She steeled herself, for she knew what was coming. She knew what she had to do. She had planned for this. She had prepared for it.

"We will be quite close in the palace, while

you protect me. I am ready to give you a preview of what we might share."

"Really?"

He stared at her stone-faced, and she took a step toward him. She had practiced this. Her hips swaying with each movement, eye contact with him never wavering. Of course, eye contact with herself in a mirror was a damn sight different than contact with the man himself. His eyes were blue. It was shocking on one with such dark hair. They were piercing, as if they could see into her soul. But he did not move.

His face was like rock. And his undoing would be that he underestimated her. His undoing would be that he did not think her an enemy.

She sighed, reached into her pocket and leaned in as if to kiss him.

Then she pulled the handkerchief out of her pocket and clapped it over his face. He removed her hand immediately, but it was too late. She had anticipated that. That he would be stronger. That his reflexes would be faster. That she would have to overdose him.

He growled and lunged toward her, knocking her back, and he came down on top of her, his hard body a heavy weight she could scarcely wiggle free of, until...

Until his muscles relaxed. Until it was clear that the chloroform had done its job.

"It is good that I planned for this."

But a one-woman kidnapping job of a very large man was not easy. Again, she had anticipated that and had brought with her a hospital gurney. In addition to a van she could load him in.

By the time she had driven to the airfield and unloaded him onto the private plane, she was feeling nearly cheerful. Had she known kidnapping her personal assassin would be quite so simple, she would have done it many years ago.

Now all that was left to do was...wait.

CHAPTER TWO

MAXIMUS WOKE READY to kill. He reached for his gun and found it wasn't there.

"I took it, obviously," came a now familiar voice.

Annick.

He immediately remembered everything that had transpired. And he had...

He was a fool. One of the most beautiful women in all the world had attempted to seduce him earlier tonight, and he had brushed her off without so much as a second glance. Annick looked at him with her round, pale eyes and had begun to walk toward him after offering her virginity, and he had stood still. He had told himself it was to see simply what she would do next, but the fact of the matter was, he had let his guard down. Which was not something he had done in his life. Not ever.

If he had, he would be dead.

No. He had done it once before. And a woman was dead because of it. But never since.

Until now.

"What the hell did you do?"

"Chloroform," she said, as if he were very stupid. "An old, but effective method to subdue. And now you are on my private plane."

"I thought you had no money."

"Not exactly. We have a limited economy in bad need of overhauling. And if selling a private plane would fix the problems I have, I would. This was obviously left over from the previous regime. The regime that no longer exists. Thank you for that. But like I said, you made this problem. I am pressed on all sides. It is not just Lackland who seeks to take advantage of my weaknesses."

"This is kidnapping," he said.

She spread her hands. "So it is. But I find I had no choice."

"I hate to tell you this, Princess, but you can't make me do what you want me to. I don't answer to anyone." He leaned back in his chair. "I'm no one's bitch. Least of all yours."

"What does this mean? *Bitch?* I do not wish you to be my 'bitch.' I wish you to be my guard and my counselor. Very clever of me. You can be *all* these things."

"Why me?"

"You know why. You are sent out by your government to depose men. Bad men. You have never once carried out an operation against the innocent, and that is not a credit to any nation, but to you."

"No," he said. "I leave the atrocities to others."

"But you don't. You don't *leave atrocities.* You handle them. You are Maximus King, this famous consultant and maker of social darlings. And you are The King, the military operative who has performed the most clean and precise removals of barbaric governments in modern history, whispered about and yet never really seen. Part of a branch of the military that may not truly exist. So many cover-ups, and coincidences, yes? And so you, specifically, are perfect for me. You will take a public position as my adviser, and given that I spent many years in a dungeon, it is perfect sense that I take an adviser. Adviser in public, guard in private. You are scary."

"Not to you, it seems."

"No, but," she said, "you are to others. And anyway, don't take it personally that you don't scare me. I am not scared by much."

She should be. She was small. Thin.

Her cheeks were round, but only because she was young. If he hadn't known about her history, then he wouldn't be able to guess. He knew about the royal family in Aillette. Their murders had been highly publicized at the time. Killed by a man who had their trust. An adviser to the King. That Princess Annick had been spared had been headline news. He had done even more digging into the royal family before he had gone to handle that bastard of a dictator last year. He knew that Annick was only twenty-two.

She was very pretty. Owed to a fine, aristocratic bone structure, and impossibly pale features. Her nose was small and pointed, her lips pale like the rest of her. Her lashes were nearly white, her eyes the softest of robin's-egg blue. She looked fragile in every way. Like contact with the sun would make her burst into flame. And she was telling him that she did not fear him.

"I lost my whole family. I lost my way of living. I was a prisoner, knowing that my only hope in all the world was, someday, for someone with more power than I to change things. Now I have power. I have a plane. I have a title. That means something. I will not sit back. Not ever again. And if I must die for my actions, then I will. But I will not wait. Not anymore. I am not a coward. And I am very angry that I have had to act the coward in order to wait until I might be most effective. You, I do not fear. I fear a life spent free where I still behave as if I am in a dungeon. That is what I fear."

He found the most grudging respect burned inside of him for Annick. Grown men feared him. As well they should. And this little Princess had kidnapped him. Something stirred inside of him, and the reaction gave him pause.

For he was not immune to feeling here.

Though for years now he had been.

Like tonight. Nothing, not a single thing, had stirred inside of him when Arianna had touched him. He couldn't get a thrill out of the job he did in the public eye. He could not even get an adrenaline rush out of pulling a gun on anyone. But this, this was interesting. This was something new.

What angered him was the fact that she thought she was in control.

"If we are to work together," he said, "you do not get the control. You cannot force me to do anything."

"Eh, but I can," she said. "With chloroform."

"You cannot possibly lug me around to every event you have planned."

She nodded her head slightly. "It is impractical, yes."

"At a certain point you will need my cooperation. And let us dispense with your threats to my family. I don't believe that you would do anything to put innocent lives in danger."

She looked regretful. "I would not *want* to."

"I don't think you will. Because that would be the real tragedy, wouldn't it? That they were able to make you into a monster such as them. Monsters who care only for their own goals."

"My goals are the welfare of my people."

"Every villain thinks they're a hero."

"Unfair," she said.

"I didn't realize we were playing fair."

"We are not playing at all," she said.

"I lie to the public to protect the images of shallow, silly people. I work in secret to rid the world of the truly vile," he said. "So the bottom line is, I'll do pretty much anything to line my pockets."

She looked at him, her eyes glittering.

"Not true," she said. "Or you would kill a bit more indiscriminately."

"I follow orders, but I make sure that I am fighting for the good of humanity. I'm not loyal to any one country, but to freedom. Human freedom. Human dignity."

"And that is what I want. Bring that to Aillette. Bring it to my people. And I will give you money."

A chance to liberate an entire country in this way was an interesting one. And in truth… He was getting tired. He was getting tired of all of it. Of the farce that he ran every day of his life. Of the wars he was waging behind the scenes.

Of seeking out atonement when he knew he could never have it.

When it came to dealing with the military, his tenure with them was much more on his own terms now than it had been in the beginning. And the unit he was part of didn't exist in an official capacity.

It was up to him what missions he did and did not take. If he wished to make Annick his mission for a time, that was up to him.

After all, if he left Annick in peril, everything he'd done up until now was a lie.

"There was an attempt on my life," she said softly. "I worry. And coming up is my coronation. I am to become Queen, not just a Princess. What will happen then, I do not know."

"You're worried they'll try again." Instantly, all of his instincts sharpened.

An attempt on her life, he could not allow. Not because he had—as she'd said—played God and upset the balance without ensuring she had adequate protection. But because if he did, then what would the point of any of it be?

To spend a life avenging one woman, while causing the harm of another.

It was everything he despised. Powerful men playing games with the world and women falling victim to them. Not because they weren't important, or smart, or strong at their core. But for want of that elusive power granted by society and the physical strength needed to fight off an enemy.

Annick needed muscle.

It could easily be him.

"Yes. The question is who do I trust, eh? I am left with a military, but who is loyal to me, really? I do not think I have the skills to ferret that out."

She didn't. Not like he did. She was small and pale and determined as hell, but she was not a military tactician. But he couldn't help her like she truly needed him to. Not with limited power.

There was a path forward that seemed clear to him, immediately.

"You might have yourself a deal," he said. "But I will have conditions."

"Yes," she said, waving a hand. "You would

not be a good mercenary if you didn't have conditions."

"I'm not *a* mercenary," he said. "Not technically. And anyway, aren't you mercenary?" he asked.

"Clearly. To an extent. Would you like a drink?" She maneuvered around the cabin of the plane, the white outfit she was wearing flowing around her body, revealing curves that he had not realized were there. She had a generous behind, and her breasts were nicely rounded.

But that didn't mean he'd take her up on her offer. There were always women.

He did not need this one.

"How do I know you won't poison it?"

"I have already proven I have a willingness to poison you. It is whether or not you decide to trust me that I can help you with. I'm willing to do what I must to get you back to my country. You are already on the plane. So, why would I bother to do anything extreme now?"

"Whiskey."

"That is this?" She held up a bottle with amber liquid inside.

"Yes."

"I have never been allowed to drink," she said. "It would not do. For I had to maintain a visage of...purity. That's what it is. Pure, snow-white Princess." She indicated her outfit. "The symbol of the spirit of Aillette." She made a tutting sound. "Such lies."

"Why did they do that?"

"Why? Because the people were restless with the monarchy, but it was not ever popular to kill my family, even in the name of a revolution. It was not that my father was such a great King, but tradition matters. And so demonstrating that I was still there, and keeping me as some kind of symbol, I think it was to give people a good feeling. Limited though my outings were. I am far too talkative."

"Shocking."

"And I suppose sometimes it worked. Though now the people are convinced I'm fragile. Even though I outlived the men who took over the country. So, who is fragile?"

"You're not fragile," he said. "Clearly."

That pleased her, he could tell. Though she

tried not to smile, she fairly beamed from the inside out.

"I'm not," she agreed. "I'm quite ruthless."

"That is apparent."

"I do what I must. I am what I've had to become to survive. You understand." The creature thought she was a sight more frightening than she was, that was obvious.

Though he did understand her. That was the problem he could understand all too well. What happened when you were left behind.

When a bullet meant for him had instead struck the woman he loved, everything had shifted. He had not been able to save Stella.

He looked at Annick. And he felt a grudging tug in his chest. As if Stella were there asking if all he could do was kill for her.

It's so easy, isn't it? To take out bad men and imagine the face of her killer every time. But that's revenge. This is a chance to actually save someone.

A vulnerable woman.

"I think we can help each other," he said.

"I knew you would see," she said, brightening.

"Yes. I see. I don't want your body," he said.

She wrinkled her nose. "Well, that is fine in any case."

She looked vaguely insulted.

"But I will take a share of what I'm investing in here." In fact, he would welcome the chance to be rid of that farce he conducted in Hollywood. It had never been a game he'd enjoyed, but lately it had grown more and more tiresome. There was a limit to how much amusement he could extract from fooling the world.

The double life he lived was wearing on him. It offended him. To go and play at rehabbing images and then go off and take down another totalitarian regime.

And all he ever did was make the smallest dent in the world. Rolling a stone up a hill forever.

And here she was, offering him a chance at redemption.

Offering him power.

"I'll help you, Annick." And he was formulating an idea of just how she could help him. She wouldn't like it. He didn't care. "You don't need my image. You need to create one of your own. I would be willing to help you with that."

"Just for money?"

He inclined his head. She didn't need to know about Stella. That was his business. His wound.

His debt.

"I am skeptical."

"I will transform you into the leader your country needs. I will cow your enemies. Better yet, you will."

He straightened as she handed him the whiskey. He swirled the liquid in the glass, doing his part to channel the Maximus King that everyone knew. It was easier. A more comfortable skin for him to act in. Annick had come face-to-face with the soldier. Few people knew of him. Even fewer who had *met* the soldier now lived to speak of it. But everyone knew this version of Maximus King. The Playboy. The one who took no one and nothing overly seriously. And why would he not take this job? It was a lark, after all.

"And if it is not fixed then? Then what? You leave—" she waved her hand "—and I am back where I was. No. I need more. I need you to stand in. I need you to keep my enemies at bay."

"Trust me, I will make Aillette into a fortress of wealth and perceived power. I will ensure you are safe, Annick. You have my word on that."

"I lived for too long, I survived for too long, to lose it all now. You cannot let it happen."

She faltered, truly faltered, and he could see now that everything Annick had done up until this point had been driven by terror. By fear. And if he were a different man, he might've felt some guilt. Might have felt some pity. Instead, he felt anger. Anger was about the only emotion he knew. It was about the only thing he could manage. Otherwise… Otherwise his chest felt hollow. Dead. It was the rage that kept him going.

His grief had burned out years ago. Like the blood that had drained from Stella as he held her in his arms. As she had died. That grief was gone.

Replaced by the poison of hatred. It fueled him. It spurred him on. It had made him lethal. It had made him useful.

The sad thing was, he knew how to play the role of Maximus King so well, because it was who he had spent the first twenty-two years of his life as. A debauched playboy. A debauched playboy who had loved precisely one person in his life more than he loved himself. And she had died in his arms.

He had been Annick's age then. And it had changed him forever.

And here Annick was, never having been silly or young. She had been a prisoner. And now she was being asked to lead a country.

"I won't. I'll protect you."

And he didn't need ask anymore why it was his responsibility. It clearly was. Nothing to be done about it.

He wasn't a good man. And he was nobody's superhero.

But when he made a promise, he kept it.

It was why he didn't make very many.

"Good." She seemed happy.

"Did you want some whiskey?"

She wrinkled her nose. "No. I think perhaps it is best that I keep my wits about me. That is a bad thing about alcohol. It takes your wits."

He chuckled. "Not a problem I have."

"Why?"

"I drink too much. And it has ceased to affect me."

She frowned. "Why?"

"Don't you have things you like to forget?"

She nodded, her expression getting very sad. "I have so many things I would like to forget. But I spent a great many years with only my own company, and I have been forced to go over the very bad things in my mind far too many times. Now... There is little point. It is too late. I have relived the past over and over again."

"I'm sorry."

Her lips curved upward. "I almost believe you."

"I am," he said, taking another drink of the whiskey.

"Do you feel it?" She touched her chest. "Here. Your sorry."

He wished he could tell her he did. That, in and of itself, was a novelty. "No. But I don't feel anything there. Except for maybe anger."

She nodded. "I am well familiar with that. It burns. I have been so angry, for so many years. Sometimes anger is the only thing that keeps you alive. And everything else… It just hurts too badly."

"Yes, you're right. Anger is easy. Anger gets things done."

"Pity is a pointless one. I tried that when I was twelve. Felt an endless amount of self-pity to go along with my grief. But then I remember, I'm the one that's alive. Not my family. So pity is not something I should feel for myself. Angry is better."

"Angry is better." He lifted his glass. "And if you would drink, we could say cheers to that."

"Say cheers?" She squinted and looked at him.

"A toast," he clarified.

"It is not toast."

"No. It's… *Salud.*"

"Right," she said, understanding.

"Where did you learn English?" he asked, intrigued by this woman who was such a strange mix of naivete and cynicism.

"From my governess. When I was a girl. So I had a lot of years when I did not use it. But I made a game in my head. To remember to speak French, and English, and German. So that I don't forget any."

"What was your life like?"

"Oh, it was not *so* bad. Except the loneliness. I had school. They could not risk me being stupid. But they also did not want me to be too educated, so they did not show me news from the world outside. I have spent the last year reading about everything that happened. Everything that happened in the world. It has been a strange and depressing time for me. But also, good."

"I imagine. That many years of world history all in one go seems a little bit extreme."

She smiled. "My life is nothing but extreme. That I can say."

"How long until we arrive in Aillette?"

"Soon. Only maybe a half hour now. I had to give you a lot of chloroform. You're very large."

He laughed. "And you are certain you wouldn't kill me?"

"I truly hope to not kill you, Maximus King. I need you too badly."

And something reached down deep in his chest just then, something he hadn't expected. Because he could not remember the last time someone had looked at him quite like that. He had been told a number of times by women that they needed him. They needed him to rehabilitate their image, which was essentially what he was going to do for Annick. That they needed him sexually. Yes, that was one of his favorites. His chest might be dead, but the rest of his body was not, and he did enjoy beautiful women. One of the perks of selecting the persona that he had chosen to carry on with his normal life.

Maximus King, the image consultant in San Diego, could have any woman he wanted. He took nothing seriously. He was charming and good in conversation. And he was even better in bed.

So yes, he was accustomed to women saying they needed him.

But not like this.

There was no greed in her eyes. No avarice.

There was an honesty there, that was what called to him. An honesty that was so dif-

ferent from anything he had been exposed
to for an age.

It was simple. And clear.

She said that she needed him, and she
meant it.

She also wouldn't hesitate to use chloroform on him if she needed to.

He didn't doubt that either. She'd do it
again.

"But you were willing to risk it."

"Well, if I could not bring you back to Aillette, then I would not have had you anyway."

"Very practical."

"I told you. I had a lot of time to think. I
have had a lot of time."

"And how did you find out that I was the
one who performed the assassination?" That
was very important. Because if he had been
made by one of his contacts, then it was
going to be a problem. There were very few
people who knew his identity. As Annick
had already said, those people had a vested
interest in the outside world not knowing that
they knew who he was. Or why they knew
him.

"I'll never tell anyone about you," she said.

"I swear it. And it is not important how I know."

"It is," he said. "I need to make sure there aren't enemies out there we both need to know about."

"No! It's only me. And I needed you. It was what I had to use against you, so I did."

"Good. You were desperate, and I will forgive you for that. But if you ever threaten my family again…"

"It is not a thing I want to do. I don't want to threaten your family. I don't wish it."

"Good."

"Ah," she said. "We are descending. I look forward to welcoming you to Aillette."

CHAPTER THREE

SHE DIDN'T KNOW why she was nervous. It was a very strange thing. To feel nervous. He was not a prisoner anymore. Sometime during the flight they had made the transition from prisoner and jail keeper into allies. And she was much more comfortable with that. She had no wish to become a jailer. Not simply because she'd had one her entire life. It was far too much work. She needed help. She did not need another project. If he had continued to resist her...

It would have been a problem.

Of course, his denial that he wanted her body had wounded her slightly, but she would not dwell on that. There was no reason for her to feel out of sorts over that exchange.

They walked into the palace, and she found she wanted him to like it. Which was quite strange. But she had changed the palace quite a bit since the other regime had fallen, and she was proud of the changes she'd made. The modernizations.

"It is a bit different since you were here last," she said, feeling proud.

He flicked a glance around the space. "I suppose it is."

"You do not remember."

"I have one job when I am sent on these missions. It is to get in and out without being detected until it is too late. That's it."

"You're cold, aren't you?"

"I have to be."

"To have a secret life? Or just to live?"

"Either. Both. Don't you think?"

"I wish I could be cold," she said, feeling a bit flat. "But I'm not. I never have been."

"Only a while ago you claimed to be ruthless," he pointed out.

It was quite annoying.

"I think they are different things. I am willing to do whatever I must for Aillette. For my people. They have suffered enough. I have suffered enough. We all have lived a collective hell. And yes, I have been willing to do what needed to be done in order to pull us from it. But there is no… There is no coldness in me. I burned with it. Like I said."

"I burn when I'm angry."

She stared at him, and suddenly, she felt warm. There was something about the look on his face, about the keenness in his blue eyes, that made her feel unsettled. That made her feel…strangely hungry. She did not like it. Did not understand it.

She squinted. "But you're cold mostly?"

Amusement tipped his mouth upward. "Mostly."

One of the women who worked on her staff, Elise, rushed up to them. "You've returned," she said, speaking in their native language, which was a dialect of French that the Parisians insisted was not French at all.

"Oui," Annick confirmed. "With Maximus King. He is my new…guard. Adviser."

"Good?" she said, phrasing it as a question.

"For the whole country," Annick said, switching to English. "He will be a great asset to Aillette. He is a businessman. And he will know how to help with the finances. He will also be exactly what we need to be taken seriously."

He chuckled. "I can't say that the world takes me seriously."

He had slipped into some sort of character. She had noticed it on the plane. Their interactions at his house and the initial interactions when he woke up were markedly different to the interactions they had after she'd given him his whiskey. She didn't know why. Except…

She knew that he had a double life. She knew that the man that he pretended to be was not the man he actually was. She knew that he was lethal. Dangerous. And that the majority of the world had no idea.

Perhaps he was playing that up, even now. And she could see why. He played an interesting and dangerous game. Being as visible as he was, conducting missions that required the utmost in discretion.

"Ready him a room," she said, and all of the women that were present in the antechamber nodded and scurried about their business. She looked to him, to see if he was impressed with the organization of the palace.

"You have a lot of women working here," he said.

"I do," she said happily. "That was one of the first changes I made, you know. For when I was here before, it was all men. Except those doing menial positions. I made a change. Women in this country who desperately needed money… I hired them. Now they can take care of themselves. If they have husbands that are cruel to them, they can leave. This is a very good thing."

"It is a good thing," he confirmed.

"I would hire men if I needed them. I am hiring you. But for the most part I find women do the work just fine."

He chuckled. "Sadly, you need a man to protect you?"

"It's sad, this thing in the world. I am not so strong."

She looked up at the ceiling. It was midnight blue marble, swirled through with bright colors. It reminded her of the painting *The Starry Night*, and she had always thought it beautiful. She had made changes to the palace, but what she'd said was true. They were not flush with money. These things were not changes she had bought. These stones had been here for centuries.

The only things that remained of her family. She had always found them soothing.

"I do not care much for men."

She had not meant to say that out loud. He was, after all, a man, and she needed his help, so perhaps it was not in her best interest to say mean things about his gender.

"You don't?"

She would have to answer for that now. "*Non*. It was not women, after all, who seized power in my country and killed my family."

"No, I suppose it wasn't. If it helps, I'm not a big fan either. I have seen a great many atrocities in this world. Most of them committed by men. So I'm with you."

"Well. I'm glad we can at least agree on that. Though I hear tell that your sex has a few things to recommend it."

"Do you?"

"I have heard. I surround myself now with many women, and we have conversations. Most of them have a fondness for at least one man in their lives. That is fair, I think. But... I do not know enough of men."

"Is that why you offered me your body?"

Heat flooded her face. "It is not a gentlemanly thing to remind me of that, I think."

"Is that so?"

She frowned deeply. "You turned me down."

"I was not aware it was a proposition, so much as a form of payment." He looked her over, his expression dispassionate. "Payment I don't require."

"Yes. That is what it was. Payment. If you don't want it, it's okay with me."

"Then you don't need to be so angry about it."

"I'm not angry," she said. "I have no anger to waste on you, in truth."

"Another very good thing, because I have a feeling that anyone who is on the receiving end of your anger is going to find himself very unhappy."

"Yes. This is true." She looked at him out of the corner of her eye. "It was a good thing they did not wish me dead. Pierre Doucet, he was a friend of my father's, and yet he killed my father, his wife and son. By order, at least. He did not spare me due to any sentimentality. I tell you this. He only wished to use me when it was convenient to show my face, and I made it hellish hard for him. I do not hold my tongue well." Anger, sadness and old fear welled up in her chest. "I might have suffered when I misbehaved, but it was worth it. A reminder that I was still me."

"They hurt you?"

She lifted a shoulder. "They killed my whole family. Stole my life. A beating here and there was nothing." She felt moisture in her eyes and hated it.

He stopped her. He did not touch her, but his gaze stopped her. And she saw there... The predator.

"I am very glad I was put on the mission to kill Pierre Doucet. I am glad I ended him."

She was not used to this. Not used to someone being so firmly on her side. "As am I."

She led him through the palace and toward the rooms that she had chosen to be his. "Here you are," she said, thankful to leave the previous subject and its accompanying heaviness in the past. "I think you will be comfortable. I have given you extra blankets."

That earned her a very long stare. "Thank you. In your chloroform kidnap, you didn't by chance happen to pick up a razor, did you? Because if not, I find myself inconvenienced."

"It is there," she said, feeling proud. "Everything you need. I anticipated that we might have difficulty. You know, I came prepared with chloroform. And I was prepared to have this room fitted out for you. With razors and anything else you might need."

"I see. And how did you, a woman who admittedly knows nothing of men, accomplish that?"

"I told you. I have women I work with who know. I do not need to know." She stepped into the room, pleased with the grandness of it. Surely he would be too. Shortly, he would be happy with this place. She might need his help, and she might need an investment, but with what she had she could offer much. The room was large, and though everything in it was old, it was competently outfitted. And she was quite pleased with it. "You will find suits."

"I don't wear suits that you buy in a store."

"We did not buy these in a store. They are made for you."

"And how," he said, "did you accomplish that?"

"I was very proud of this. I called your sister."

He frowned. "You called my sister? Which sister?"

"Minerva. I called Minerva, and I told her that I was designing you a suit, but could not get a hold of you, and that I needed information from your tailor, which she gave to me. And then I got your measurements."

"You are a stunning little weasel—do you know that?"

"What does this mean? *A weasel.* I'm not a weasel."

"Sneaky. Weasels are sneaky."

"Oh, yes," she said, feeling pleased with that. "I am sneaky. So. A weasel it is."

"You know," he said, pausing at the center of the room. "You're the only one who knows. The only one who knows who I am. Everyone else in this world knows Maximus King, and some might know about The King, that much-whispered-about super soldier. But they don't know both."

"*I* know both. Though what I do wonder

is if actually no one knows either one. Do you know?"

"What kind of question is that?"

She shrugged. She shouldn't keep staring at him. He really was desperately handsome, and it was throwing her off-balance.

He was the kind of man who made a woman do foolish things. Those were the kinds of things she knew about from her staff. They had become her friends. And she could admit she had hired women her age so that she might have some friends.

She had missed a lot of life.

And she listened as they sighed and moaned and talked about all the ways they were fools for the men they claimed to love. Annick had found it incredibly off-putting. But she was also curious; she couldn't deny it. She did not know men. And that was... It was a difficult realization.

She had lived around them and been kept by them, but men to her were nothing more than imposing physical presences. Every one of her captors had disgusted her. Every one. But what she felt when she looked at Maximus was not disgust. Not even close. She had a feeling it connected up to all that long-suffering sighing of the women she knew. But she also could not quite imagine what it would mean. Physical intimacy like that. She knew what it was, in the practical sense. Knew what it was physically. But she did not really understand why a person would do it.

She looked at him, and heat stole over her body.

Do you really not understand?

"An honest one," she said. "The man you were at your house, the man when you woke up on the plane, the man you are now, they are not all the same man. So I wonder. Do you know which is real? Are any of them real?"

"Here's a hint. I was *this* man once. This one. Maximus King. Charming and easy to be around. With absolutely no blood on his hands." He paused for a moment. "Until I wasn't."

"I see. Something happened to you."

"Yes. Something happened to me."

Except, she had the sense that that wasn't strictly true either. That he was holding something back, even saying that much.

"Get your suit," she said. "And dress for dinner. You will join me and we will go over the timeline for my plans. I am eager to speak of such things."

Then she turned and left him there, feeling trembly and shaky and not entirely certain what was happening inside of her.

But it didn't matter. What mattered was that in just two weeks, she would be Queen. And Maximus King was here to protect her.

She had done it.

That was all that mattered.

CHAPTER FOUR

THE SUIT FIT, which irritated him more than he would like to admit. That the little devil surprised him was also more irritating than he would like to admit.

There was something about her. About the way she asked questions. The way she talked about her life. He found it difficult to be unaffected by her.

What he was good at was showing no emotion at all. Betraying nothing of what was going on inside of him. And so, when she had spoken again of offering her body, he had been able to remain outwardly impassive.

Even while inside he had felt more than a stirring of interest.

Come to dinner.

She was issuing commands that he had no reason to deny. Which would most certainly put her in a false mind of just how in control she was.

He could walk away from all of this at any time. This insanity. This farce.

But nothing has held your interest this long for...

Well, that was the issue. Nothing had. He often wondered if it was even possible for him to feel anything again. And then she had shown up. She had made him feel... Well, she had made him feel.

And she had managed to fill a closet up with custom suits that fit.

That in and of itself earned his acceptance of the dinner invitation, he should think.

The palace itself was old. Not crumbling, but definitely showing its age. Fortunately, it was put together with precious stones and metals, and those things tended to gather color and richness as they aged. Tended to find a new sort of life.

The palace was no exception. The jade and amethyst, emerald and ruby, was only that much more entrancing now.

And if he were a man whose head was turned by such things, he would be in awe.

But no. The gemstones did not do it. However, when he walked into the dining room and saw her, he felt his blood begin to heat.

She was different than when he had seen her last. She had been dressed all in white before, a flowing pantsuit, with her pale blond hair caught in a knot at the base of her neck.

Now she was wearing a green gown cut to show off her curves. Her blond hair was loose, spilling over bare shoulders, falling like corn silk over her breasts. Everything about her looked soft. And he knew that wasn't the case. So the artistry that must've gone into making her appear that way was surely a thing of great mastery.

The makeup around her eyes was gold, her lips crimson.

"I'm glad you could join me," she said.

"You will recall it was more a demand than a request."

"I did half expect to have to drag you out of your bedroom."

"I was banking on you not wishing to chloroform me in order to accomplish the task.

But then, I also don't see the point of turning down a free meal."

"A smart man. Very smart. And good."

"No," he said. "Not good."

"I meant only that it is good you are smart. I did not mean you were good. You are, I know, a killer."

"Yes," he said.

"Your family does not know."

"No," he said, taking a seat at the head of the long table. "My family does not know. Nor will they."

"Perhaps we could invite some of them to my coronation. Under the pretense you are my consultant. It will be advantageous for me to have a connection to Monte Blanco. And to your brother-in-law, Prince Javier."

"Yes. I'm sure it will be advantageous for you. It's a shame he's so busy with his new wife, or you could've kidnapped him."

"It is true," she said. "He would have been most convenient. A spare, no official position in his country, but raised to be royal. Also, he is the captain of the guard." She frowned. "His brother, though, I hear has an ill humor. He would not have liked me to kidnap him."

"You know a lot about my brother-in-law."

"Of course. It pays to know these things. As I said, I have spent the last year going over everything."

"What have you learned?"

"Everything about world events." She squared her small shoulders. "You know they shielded me from many things. What was happening out there. And I wanted to learn all of it, and I did. And I thought…it would make the blank spaces in my mind feel full." She blinked. "It did not." She didn't speak for a long moment. "I wonder… I wonder. I would like…some time to learn more about myself."

"What do you mean by that?"

She shrugged, in that rather careless way she had. "You know, I have had so much decided for me. And even now, I know so little. I wish to do things like choose my own clothes. As an example. I hate everything that was bought for me. So, when the regime fell, I had my staff choose clothes for me. But I don't know if it is what I like. I don't know how to know what it is I like. Same with food. I did not keep the same menus, but I went back to what my mother and father made. Some I like. Some..."

"So what you're telling me is you know a lot about the state of the world, but not what you want to eat for dinner."

"It is exactly this," she said. "Some things I know... Some things I don't."

"I..." He found himself speechless, which was...not something that he could remember happening. Except he suddenly realized that he wasn't sure what he liked anymore either. He played a part. Slipped that role on like a second skin. He drank to excess in public because Maximus King would. He had supermodels on his arm because it was what Maximus King would do. Some grotesque version of himself that he imagined might have existed had he never known Stella. Had he never been in love.

A reckless playboy who cared only about appeasing his own appetites. But for someone who indulged as richly as he did in the hedonistic things of this world, he could not say that he loved them. He drank whiskey on the plane because whiskey was what he drank, not because he loved whiskey particularly. And he found the sort of beauty Annick possessed to be far more compelling than the beauty on any of those supermodels. As for food…

He ate what was served to him. He did not consider it much.

"What is it?"

"That will be our first step, Annick. We will find out what you like to eat. How do you summon your staff?"

"A bell," she said. She looked very pleased, and she produced a small silver bell.

"Ring it."

She did so. And three women appeared, with their hair in low, neat ponytails, their clothing all the same, black from head to toe.

"We need food. Food from restaurants in the city. Whatever was being cooked tonight, bring that too, but bring a variety. Annick— Princess Annick—needs to try some things."

"What are you doing?" she asked.

"It does not do, Annick, for a Queen to not know her own mind. You need to know what you like. Everything you like. Because it is the job of those around you to make you happy, to make you comfortable, and if you do not know what you want, how can you give easy commands? If you cannot give easy commands…you don't look like you're in charge."

She looked like she was considering this. "Okay."

"Mostly," he said, "if you don't enjoy things, you will become cold and hard and dead inside."

"What? Like you?" She asked it with some humor, but she had no idea.

"Yes," he said. "Like me."

She looked slightly abashed. "Sorry," she said.

"Are you going to say that you didn't mean it?"

"Oh, no," she said. "I very much meant it. Only I am sorry that I said it. I'm very out of practice with talking to people I don't hate."

He laughed, the bubble of humor in his chest entirely unexpected.

"Are you?"

"I have made friends," she said. "Here on my staff. But it is a learning process."

"I see."

"Yes, I think you do."

"Regrettably, talking to people that you hate will be part of the position that you occupy. I have to talk to people I hate all the time."

"As a hit man or as an image consultant?"

"As an image consultant. I don't talk to anyone in my other job. And you had better be careful about where and how you speak of such things. I'll ask again—how did you find out about me?"

She shifted. "No one knows who 'The King' is. I know. They know you are coming for them, but they did not know from where. Me, I listen. I have nothing else to do but listen. I collect information as I can. And somehow, it all just fit."

"How did you know about me at all?"

"Your sister Violet. I was fascinated by her. By this woman from California, who married a Prince and helped reform a country. After all, is that not what I must do?"

"Yes. Though I think you must give her husband and his brother some of the credit for the reformation of their country."

"Yes. I did not say they don't get credit. But I was intrigued by the way bringing in an outsider could help. That is when I started looking at you. And that is when I realized. That you are The King."

"Again, how?"

"Connecting dots."

"No one else has connected those dots."

"When you are a prisoner for so very long, and cut off from so many things, your other senses become heightened. And you learn how not to be stupid. And so, I am not stupid."

"Tell me."

"I saw you."

His breath left his body. She looked up at him, her pale eyes glittering. "I was hiding. In the dungeon. I heard footsteps. And I am not a fool. When you are kept locked away, you have very few options when it comes to deciding when you want to speak to someone or not. So, often, I'm quiet. I hid in the corner. I heard you. And I saw you. But you did not see me. I was in the darkness, and I saw you. Your eyes."

"My face was covered."

She shook her head. "Doesn't matter. I saw your eyes, and though you did not see me, I felt it. Like lightning here," she said, touching her stomach. "When I saw you in your house, it was the same. I've never seen eyes like lightning."

He gritted his teeth, holding back what he thought might be the truth. It wasn't so much that she *recognized* him as she was attracted to him. And who would have ever thought that his undoing would become some virgin trapped in a dungeon *recognizing* him because he made her heart beat faster.

"But you must have known before you came."

"I suspected. I suspected from seeing pictures, yes. But I knew for sure when I went to your house."

"And if you had been wrong?" he asked.

"I might have kidnapped you anyway. Either way, either persona, is of use to me."

"You *are* ruthless, aren't you?"

His proclamation seemed to cheer her immensely. "I said so. I don't lie, Maximus. I tried. It would have been easier were I proficient at it. I might have been let out of the dungeon more. I might have been beaten less. And now here I am, free. I *hate* lies. If I am to be the best Queen, then I cannot lie."

"Life is a bit grayer than that, Annick. I hate to inform you."

"Eh…" she said, that nasal sound of dismissal she seemed quite fond of. "I'm tired of gray. I'm tired of the dark."

She would not like, then, what he was planning. But she would have no choice.

She'd brought him here.

But he would be the one to decide how it went.

Then the doors to the dining hall flung open and in came trays laden down with food.

For now, he would let her eat.

"And here we are," he said. "Your dinner is served."

Annick stared at the food that had now been laid out on the table, and then she looked back at the man who was responsible for ordering it.

"This is nice."

She foolishly found that she wanted to cry. She had read once, in her studies, that small kittens that were kept in cages from the time they were born still saw the bars in front of them even when they were removed, and staring at this feast laid out in front of her, she had to wonder if she had been seeing bars where there were none.

If she still treated herself as a prisoner. She often kept to corners of the palace. She did not indulge herself overmuch. Some of it was wanting to preserve that which she felt was important. Her integrity. Some of it was being afraid that wanting too much would make her little more than a dictator.

But… He had brought all this food from restaurants run by her people. It surely benefited them that this money had been spent.

Her stomach growled. She was hungry. And she was…delighted.

"I have never seen so much food." She frowned. "Except I must have. In the early days of the palace. I was twelve when that ended. And I know I have memories from before. But…"

"It's hard," he said, his voice surprisingly tender. "When memories from before are too good."

She nodded. "Yes, it is not bad memories that I turn away from. The bad reminds me why I keep going. It always has. It is a terrible thing to think of my parents dying. But their deaths reminded me of why I lived. But remembering how happy we were…that was too painful. Well and truly."

"Annick," he said. "You can enjoy the food."

She practically fell upon it then. She was starving. But it had more to do with everything else than it did actual physical hunger.

She piled the plate high with salad, french fries, bread, pastry. Steak.

"Quite an assortment."

"It is what I want. Isn't that what this is about? What I want?"

"Yes."

She suddenly felt a bit bratty and quite self-indulgent. But she wanted it. For just these few moments.

"Eat pastries first," she said.

"Is that by royal command?"

"Unless you don't want to. Eat what it is you want. But do not let protocol stop you from eating the pastries."

"Annick, protocol never stops me from anything."

She studied him. "No. I expect not."

She had done so much reading about him. About The King and about Maximus. And she wondered which bits and pieces were true. She wondered if he was half so…wicked as the tabloids claimed.

And then she wondered why she was quite so interested. Yes, she had been prepared to offer her body to him. The very idea made her warm now. What would she have been? If she had been free? What foods would she have liked? Would she have had a score of lovers by now?

She very much liked the look of this man. She wanted to touch him. It stood to reason that if she were around other men who possessed a certain level of attractiveness, she might wish to touch them too. And if she had full freedom…she might have.

She turned her focus back to the food, but she could feel his eyes on her.

"You must realize, Annick, that your plan will not work."

She looked at him again. "What?"

"Adviser. Guard. These are not official titles. It is not a statement. It is not strong."

"And you think you can do better than this plan?"

"I know I can. It isn't enough to have me by your side. You want 'The King'? I will be the King, Annick. But you will be my wife."

CHAPTER FIVE

"FOOLISHNESS!" SHE SAID, without even thinking. "I cannot *marry* you."

"And why not?"

"You said you didn't want power," she said, narrowing her eyes. "A lie. You are making the ultimate power grab now that you are here."

"You brought me here—you can hardly accuse me of engineering it. But think about it. What stronger stance will you take as a Queen than having a King beside you? And I can protect you, truly protect you. I can be in your chamber at night."

Heat crackled up her spine. "You said you did not want my body."

"I do not. But this is a traditional country. Do you think you won't create rumors by bringing me here? Me? With my reputation?"

Her eyes went narrow and bright. "Okay. I see. But…but to what end?"

"*Any* end. The end that makes the most sense."

"And what do you get out of it?"

"The good I can do commanding an army outstrips what I can do alone. Don't you think?"

"For how long?" she asked, her chest squeezing tight. "How long would we have to…?"

"For life. A royal marriage cannot be anything else, but we can live separate lives."

"And…and children?" she asked, her throat dry as sandpaper.

"There will have to be children. For your kingdom." His words were like stone. "But no need to concern ourselves with them for now, don't you think?"

She shook her head, her ears buzzing like they were filled with bees. "Years."

"Years," he agreed.

"I am angry with you," she said, her heart thundering hard. "Because this is not stupid. Not foolish. But I do not want it."

"I didn't want to come here in the first place, but you brought me. If you bring a lion into your house, you cannot be angry when he goes on the hunt, can you?"

She sat there, her scalp and cheeks burning with shame.

"What are you thinking about?"

"Sex," she responded.

"A topic you seem invested in."

Her face was like fire now. "Well, you asked me for marriage, and that means it matters. Is what they say about you true?"

"Who, and what?"

"The papers. They say you're very wicked. That you...that you have an insatiable appetite for women. In a sexual sense."

"I understood what you meant."

"Well, I find that I'm curious. If it is true."

"No."

Her stomach felt something strange. It was a lot like disappointment, though it shouldn't have been. "Oh."

"I'm not insatiable. I suppose, if you ask some, I'm wicked. But...insatiable implies a bit more passion than perhaps I feel."

"You are not passionate?"

He looked down the table. "You're hungry, yes?"

"Yes, I am hungry. Maybe five times a day. I eat small amounts at a time typically."

"Sex is another appetite," he said.

The words were flat, and practically spoken. And she did not think they should make her stomach go tight.

"When I am hungry, I eat. When I want a woman, I seek one out. I do not see the point in denying hungers. But I'm not a glutton."

"Hmm," she mulled. "Perhaps I am."

"Do you think?"

She looked at her plate of food, which was half-demolished. And she looked at what remained. "Yes. I think I might be. I have been denied, and this is all here. And I want it all. Everything I have missed."

"You think it will be the same with other things?"

"I'm beginning to wonder." She frowned. "Will you have love affairs?"

"I do not intend that we should be beholden to only each other," he said. "Be as gluttonous as you wish."

"So, you would have me take lovers, then?"

"Eat your food, Annick."

His patience with her was wearing very thin. She could see.

"I suppose I must learn to be less forthright."

"Probably."

"It's just I'm very tired of this."

"I'm sorry, but a life in the public eye is to an extent signing up for a *life* of subterfuge. This is something I know a lot about. And you did not answer me."

"This is not fair. I want to be *me*, and I want to be free, but that is not… It is not possible, is it?"

"No. For a life of public service means always carrying yourself with a certain amount of diplomacy."

"Yes. Though…"

"There is no *though*," he said. "If you wish to be taken seriously as a leader, if you wish to be seen as something other than a child, caught in the center of all this, if you wish to be a Queen, to escape the tragedy that has happened to you, then you have to behave like any leader would be expected to behave."

"I have done," she said, feeling irritated now. And exceptionally hard done by. "I went and kidnapped you, did I not? I behaved as a leader would. I refused to subject my country to further unrest by keeping us at risk. I am strong."

"Then you will learn to show it in a way that the world recognizes. You asked me to come and help you. I have offered marriage. Now, don't resist me."

She let out a particularly delicious French curse and then took another bite of delicious pastry. At least her fury paired well with butter.

"Don't take it personally."

"I'm tired," she said. "That is all."

"Go to bed."

"No. I'm tired of my life. For a moment, I looked at all this food and I thought, why should I not have everything I want? But then you reminded me. You reminded me that I must be, in some way, still not me."

"You can be you. With the friends that you have here in the palace. It's just that with diplomats you are going to have to endeavor to behave in a certain fashion."

"All right. I endured prison these many years. Why not more?"

"It is prison?" he asked. "To be married to me?"

"I do not know." She looked at the table laid out before her. She would have had to choose a husband someday. And he was a good choice. The idea made her skin feel oversensitive. "No. I suppose it's not."

"And a gentle reminder, that you have taken me prisoner."

"You have agreed," she said.

"In the way that you agreed?"

She waved a hand at him. "Don't do that. Don't try to paint yourself as some sort of victim, when we both know you're not. You would not stand for it. You have agreed to help me, and I cannot say that I know why, but I do know this—you have chosen to. I was prepared to fight to bring you over to my side, but I did *know* that I needed to bring you to my side. I knew that I was not going to be able to hold you as a prisoner."

"Indeed, Annick."

"Don't you ever feel tired? Two lives. It's too many lives. I did not even do it so successfully, and it was too many for me."

"It is not," he said. "Because I am living

one of them for someone who cannot live at all. Perhaps if you thought of it that way, it would help."

Her heart twisted, the sympathy that she felt surprising her. She had lost so much it was rare that anyone else's loss touched her. Then again, she didn't often sit and speak to another person. Not like this.

"Who did you lose?"

"It doesn't matter. *Who* doesn't matter— not anymore. But dedicating my life to re- moving men from the world who create destruction? That is a fitting tribute to their memory. Trust me on that."

"It is strange, is it not? That sometimes to become avengers of atrocities we must com- mit some of the same. You know, me kid- napping you."

"We do what we must. I cannot despise you too greatly because of that."

"I find I cannot despise you, this marriage bargain notwithstanding. But then, it was never my goal."

"What is your favorite?"

She looked at all the food. "I couldn't choose."

"You must have a favorite."

"Choice. That's my favorite."

He smiled and nodded slowly. "That is a good answer."

CHAPTER SIX

HE SLEPT WELL in the palace, and there was something surprising about that. It was strange to be here as himself, when the last time, he had been here as The King.

He looked in the closet, shaking his head. The way that Annick had gone about procuring a wardrobe for him was one of the most ridiculous things he'd ever heard. But also, ingenious, and it was true what he'd said to her last night. He had to respect her determination. She was a strong, feral creature, and if Stella had wanted him to pour his energy into anything, it would've been helping Annick.

It was not all truism that drove him, not really. There was something more difficult to pin down. He had been working for years now to try and make Stella's death mean something. The problem was, there was not much in the way of meaning to be found in the death of a beautiful young woman caught in a firefight between businessmen that she should've had nothing to do with. He was not a man who sat. He was not a man who stood idly by and let things happen, and he had been unable to do anything when it had mattered most.

He dressed in a suit and marveled at the fact that it really did fit perfectly.

He paused for a moment, guessing where he thought Annick might be.

And for some reason, he knew she would still be in her room.

There'd been something watchful about her in the large dining room. She had said she was not accustomed to big meals like that, and what he wondered was if Annick was still uncomfortable in large spaces. She had been kept in a dungeon most of her life, so he could see why. He paused in front of a woman wearing what he took to be the palace uniform. "Princess Annick's room?"

She eyed him warily. "If Annick has not given you the location of her chambers..."

"I will find it, thank you."

If he were Annick, he would have put him

close by. She would want him to be near enough to be convenient. Perhaps far enough to feel safe.

Then there was the simple question of where the primary bedchamber in the house was most likely to be located. He paused at the end of the corridor. At the double doors there.

"There you are." And then he flung them open.

"Eh!" She made a sharp exclamation and scrambled back on the bed, covering herself with her sheets. Annick had her hair in a braid and was wearing what appeared to be an extremely virginal white nightgown. She had coffee and pastries around her.

"Good morning," he said.

"I did not say you could come in."

"No. You didn't." He shrugged carelessly. "But I didn't ask."

"Treason," she said.

"To enter the Princess's bedchamber unannounced? My *fiancée's* bedchamber."

"I may have agreed," she said, sniffing loudly. "But it is not announced."

"I assume you will announce it soon."

"Indeed," she said. "At the coronation. I made a plan of it last night." She gestured toward a notebook on the bed, and he could not explain it, but his stomach went hollow.

She was…*cute*. And he could not remember the last time he'd found anything or anyone *cute*.

"Why do you eat in here?"

"I like it. I did not have a real bed for a great many years. This is one of my favorite places to be. Bed."

She looked at him, and then suddenly color flooded her face.

And he felt an answering desire tug low in his gut.

What he'd said to her last night was true.

Sex for him was simply an appetite to be sated.

He was not the prowling, ravenous wolf that the tabloids made him out to be.

He had loved only one woman in his life, and he had loved her very dearly. They had been young, and while sex had been a part of their relationship, it had been…sweet. He had not been Stella's first lover, but her second, and she his. Their lovemaking had hardly been the kind that rattled the walls.

But they had cared for each other. At first, he had thought that maybe women just wouldn't be a part of his life, but it had gotten to a point where it didn't seem like there was any reason to not have sex. His heart could not be touched. That was simply a fact. His body, though…

There was no point making it an issue. No point making it much of anything.

Annick unfortunately engaged, not his heart, but his sense of obligation. And along with it, desire. This was not as simple as he liked his attractions to be.

They would have to have children, for the sake of the kingdom. And what was marriage to him? Nothing.

But he would have her gently. With care for what she'd suffered. And it wouldn't be about desire.

He would have control.

"Is that so?"

"Yes. Would you like a pastry?"

"Thank you," he said. "Though I would prefer coffee."

"I have that as well."

"An extra cup?"

"I have that too," she said. "Coffee service can be made in my room." She looked very pleased with that.

He crossed the space and found the coffee station. Where he poured himself a cup of black brew, then went and sat on the end of her bed.

She turned pink, all the way to the roots of her hair. "What is my lesson today, then?"

"What lesson do you feel is the most important?"

"Well. At the coronation, I will need to know dancing. I do not know dancing. I will also have to carry on conversation with people I don't know. And... I will need clothes."

"A stylist can be employed for that, and they will help you figure out what it is you like. And combine it with what it is you want to say."

"What does this mean?"

"Your clothes send a message. As you mentioned to me earlier, they liked to dress you in white because it sent the message that you were pure. An unsullied figurehead. In that same way, you will be making statements now."

"I need to look powerful. Confident. I don't want to look pure. I want to look like a warrior."

"Then all you need to do it is to speak to the stylist about it."

"All right. Dancing, can you help me with that?"

"Yes. More than that, I can help you project the right feelings. In the world we live in now, where pictures are taken constantly, if you're going to be pretending to be something you're not, you have to be very good at it."

"Is that how you ended up consulting people on image?"

"No. It could've been anything. It is something I slipped into and I am good at it. Very good. I've spent my life in Southern California, around people who are nothing but image conscious. And yes, I had to learn to fit in. I had to learn to pretend that I was one of them." His chest went tight. "That I was like my father."

"Your father…"

"Robert King. Self-made businessman extraordinaire. Not as entirely on the up-and-up as he would like the world to believe." His father had secrets. Secrets he knew would hurt his whole family. Secrets that had already hurt the innocent. "My father is an expert at looking like he belongs."

"Is that where you learned it from?"

Perhaps it was simply in his blood. "I don't know that I learned it from him, but I discovered what a necessity it was by being his son."

"I see." He did not think she did. But it didn't matter. She didn't need to see.

"Get dressed," he said.

"I do not take orders," she said, narrowing her eyes and curling her fingers around her coffee cup like claws. "I'm to be Queen."

Half his mouth lifted. It might have been a smile, though he hadn't decided to do it, which was strange. "A boon for you, surely."

"Indeed."

"But for now, you are only a Princess. And I," he said, turning that half smile into his best grin, the one that he knew made women flutter. The one that spurred every tabloid to print photos of him. "I am The King and you will do what I say. That is what you brought me here for, am I correct?"

"To do *my* bidding," she said, pulling her knees up to her chest, the thin white material on her gown pulling down, exposing the plump, firm lines of her breasts.

He could see her nipples through the fabric. He would've said that he was a damn sight too jaded to get excited over a shadow of areola, but apparently when it came to Annick he was anything but immune.

He straightened the cuffs on his suit jacket. "Annick, I do no one's bidding. I do not take jobs I don't see as important. Now, you listen to me. I am not staying in Aillette forever. We might marry, but I will go on with my life. I will not be here to prop you up forever. That means you must learn to stand on your own feet. Congratulations, you managed to get me to the palace. Now make use of me. Do not be stubborn. Do not fight simply because you spent years being unable to fight. Because you felt weak. You weren't weak. If you were weak, you would be dead. You wouldn't be here. You hate that you had to hide pieces of yourself, but it kept you alive. You hate that you had to play a game, but it's why you're here. So now you will play a new game. And you will let me teach you the rules."

"I don't like this," she said, looking at him out of the sides of her eyes.

Wretched creature that she was, he imagined she had disliked a great deal in her life. "I don't care. If you will not work with me, if you will not do what I say, then I will walk out right now."

"I will have the guards seize you."

"I would hate to hurt your guards."

"You have no weapons," she said.

He fixed his gaze on her. "Annick, do you honestly think that I require weapons? A gun is a useful prop, but a man must know how to take care of himself. A man must know how to contain all the danger he possesses in his own body. Myself, I can seduce or I can kill…with just my hands. I don't require weapons. As you observed, I am both Maximus King and The King. I could be anything I choose."

"You will *not* kill my guards," she said.

"I certainly wouldn't want to. But if I decide to leave, I will leave. And only God will be able to help those who stand in my way." He looked at her. "Now, get dressed."

CHAPTER SEVEN

ANNICK WAS STILL stewing by the time she made her way downstairs. She had put on a pair of black wide-legged trousers and a navy blue shirt. Mostly because she knew that he expected her to come down in a dress, given that he was already clad in a suit in the early hours of the morning speaking of dance lessons.

So, she did not comply, because it was the only power she could find in the moment.

She had the terrible feeling that she was outclassed in about a thousand ways as she walked down the stairs that led to the ballroom.

Perhaps it was all a false sense of security. Being able to take him from California in the first place. She had gotten the upper hand, but she had the sense that she hadn't had the true scope of what was happening. She had engaged in a battle and won a tentative victory. But this was a war, and Maximus had the controlling power.

She'd wanted that power. Finally. To be in total control of all that happened around her, and by engaging Maximus, she'd entered into a devil's bargain where control wasn't possible. Even though he was fighting for her, he had still superseded her.

So, small rebellions it would be.

Her heart fluttered strangely as she approached the ballroom, and she took a breath, pushing both doors open and making a rather dramatic entrance. He did not even give her the satisfaction of looking surprised.

"It took you long enough. Come over here."

"I don't think you understand. I don't like orders," she said, fixing him with her most narrow stare.

"I don't think *you* understand. I don't care what you like. You asked for a very specific thing—in fact, you demanded it. Now you must face the consequences of your own actions. You were a prisoner for a great many years, subject to the whims of other people, so perhaps you have forgotten what it means to have agency."

"I have always had it. No one could ever get in here," she said, tapping her temple.

"Perhaps. But I meant in the real world, where real actions take place outside of here." He tapped the same spot she had just tapped. And she flinched. His touch aroused strange sensations between her legs, and she didn't like it. "There are real consequences. If you are going to run around acting tough enough to take me on, then you have to be prepared for what comes of it."

"Threats," she said. "Many, many threats. And yet here you are, standing in the middle of my ballroom."

"It would not do to let you die. It would not do to let you fail."

"Why?" she asked, feeling emboldened. "What is this sudden caring that you have for if I live or die?"

"I'm not a monster," he said.

"Are you not? For I was under the impression that you were."

"There is one code that I have, one thing I live by. I will not let innocent women be destroyed. I will not do it. I will not take part in it. I will not allow it. If there is a chance for me to stop atrocities being committed against the innocent, then I will. It is the only thing that keeps me from being a monster. And you should be grateful that it's a vow I've taken. It's why I won't just leave you. It's why I have agreed to help."

"Why?"

"That, my dear, is none of your blessed business."

"And why not?"

"You might have discovered some of my secrets, but you don't get to know me." He leaned in, and the scent of him wound itself around her, made it difficult for her to breathe or think. Made her head fuzzy. "No one knows me."

He moved away from her, and she did not find it any easier to breathe now. She could still smell the vague impression of him. Skin and cologne and something very uniquely him.

"You don't get to know me either," she said.

He chuckled, and then he wrapped his arms around her and pulled her up against his hard chest. "You don't know yourself, darling." He moved one hand to her lower back and grabbed her hand in his other, holding it outstretched. "Now, we learn to dance."

He moved her over the ground like she weighed nothing, his strength calling to something inside of her that she could not quite grasp. His strength making her feel vulnerable and empowered all at once.

She had never felt anything quite like this before. The sensations of being held in a man's arms. She resented that he made her feel this.

But then…

She met his gaze and her stomach turned over.

She could read nothing there. It was impossible. His mouth was set into a grim line, his jaw forbidding and square, the stubble that darkened it making him look even more dangerous and disreputable.

She sort of wished he were the ravening wolf she'd been led to believe he was from the tabloid stories. Because if he were, then he might have done something to answer the restless calling that rose up between her thighs. If he were, then maybe none of these strange feelings inside of her would be questions. They would simply be action.

She was supposed to be learning to dance, but what she was learning was the unexpected joy in feeling feminine and fragile. It had always been something she despised.

She was small, and it meant she could not fight back physically against the men who kept her imprisoned. The men who oppressed her people and her country.

She had taken no joy in the things that made her a woman. In her softness. Had never found her breasts to be at all useful.

But he made them feel heavy. Aching with desire to be touched.

Suddenly, their existence seemed to make sense, and that was a wholly awing and unexpected sensation.

But he was controlled. Dispassionate. And he seemed not to feel any of the things that she did. None of the sparks that rioted over her skin as he shifted his hold on her.

She had forgotten she was learning to dance. She was simply following his movements. Her feet somehow naturally gliding over the floor in a rhythm, following along with his own.

"You've done this before," he said.

She shook her head. "No."

Yet as he said that, she had a memory. A faint one. A small one.

Of laughing and twirling in the ballroom, standing on her father's feet.

She pushed it away.

"No," she said, her throat going tight. "No. There was never any dancing."

"Well, you are very good at it."

"Why compliment me?" She looked at him, feeling angry. Angry that he was trying to bring memories up inside of her when she would just as soon not have any. "You hate me."

"I don't hate you. I find that I hate the world that brought you to the place you're in now. But not you."

"Disappointing."

She didn't know why that made her angry. Only that it did. Perhaps because it would be satisfying if he felt something as hard-edged for her as hatred.

Because she felt like she was being cut

open from the inside, being held in his arms, and he was like marble. Unmoved. In... everything.

"Don't be petulant, Annick. It does not suit you."

"Don't try to be kind, Maximus. It does not suit *you*."

"I have never met a woman filled with so much spite when she's getting exactly what she wants."

"And I have never met a man who so determinedly did not live up to his reputation. *Disappointing*."

He cocked his head to the side, his eyes keen. And suddenly she felt naked in a way that was disconcerting but not entirely unpleasant. "What exactly is disappointing you?"

"I don't know, but you are legendary. Playboy. Soldier. Either identity. I would have expected you to be something a bit more... I don't know. *Dangerous*."

And suddenly, she found herself being propelled back, her shoulders butting up against the wall of the ballroom. "Am I not dangerous enough for you?"

She huffed. "I have subdued you."

And that was when she felt the air between them change. His lips curved into a half smile, the light in his eyes turning into a blue flame.

His hand drifted from where it held hers, slowly, the tips of his fingers gliding over the tender skin of her wrist, up to the curve of her elbow. "Subdued?"

They drifted along to her shoulder, across the line of her collarbone, to the base of her throat. And then he raised his hand slowly and rested it on her neck. He did not squeeze. Did not tighten his hold at all—rather, he simply let it rest there. But she could feel the danger. The threat.

And winding through it, as if it were a threefold cord, eroticism.

Something that made her skin crackle. That made her nipples tighten and that place between her legs go soft and damp.

"You only think that because you still labor under the delusion that you have captured me. You invited me in. I am in your palace. Ready to take the position of power that you have offered to me. Nothing will happen here that I do not decide. Do not mistake control for subjugation, Annick. It would be a grave mistake on your part."

Then he released his hold on her, and she found herself still there, pinned to the wall, her heart beating wildly.

She didn't know what had just happened.

She had made a study out of engaging in power plays that the other party did not know they were involved in. But this was an open war for power, naked and on display.

He was right. She had invited him into the palace. She had offered him carte blanche. And she didn't actually know what he would do with it.

He claimed that he would protect her. That he would help her.

But he was clearly going to do it only on his terms.

And for the first time she did wonder if she were foolish.

If she had sought emancipation at the hands of a man who only knew how to control.

His business training women how to control their images—that was a facade. That was a piece of him that wasn't real or true.

So who knew what he was actually doing. What the end result truly was.

Remember what you want. Remember what you need.

Yes. She would do well to remember that. Who she was. What she had come to him for.

And suddenly, she was not content to allow him to have the final say in this interaction.

And so she flung herself away from the wall, wrapped her arms around his neck and crashed her lips against his.

And the world burst into flame.

CHAPTER EIGHT

HER KISS WAS unpracticed. Unskilled.

She kissed him like a girl might kiss her very first crush. With desperation and earnestness, closed mouth and frozen, even while her body vibrated with energy.

And he...

He felt a molten flame melting in his stomach that was unlike anything he could remember experiencing.

Her breasts were firm and lush, pressed against the hardness of his chest, and his hand found its way down to the rounded curve of her ass, squeezing tight as she continued to kiss him.

"Open for me," he growled, angling his head and pushing his tongue between her lips.

She gasped, but the gasp accomplished his command. Turned shock into obedience. And he took advantage of it.

A whimpering cry rose up in her throat as he slid his tongue slowly against hers, teaching her the deep, slick rhythm that could exist at the center of a kiss.

Even if she had not already told him she was an innocent, he would know.

There was no disguising it. She had been angry when she'd thrown herself at him, but the anger had evaporated. Replaced by wonder, curiosity and arousal that she did not have the skills to hide.

But there was something about that. About the genuine nature of her reaction that made it impossible for him to resist.

And if he should, he could not remember why.

Really? This woman, this sad, desperate woman, who has been kept captive all these years, and you can't think of a single reason why you shouldn't be kissing her right now?

Control.

The word penetrated his lust-fueled haze. And for the first time in longer than he could remember he felt ashamed.

Ashamed of what he had done, ashamed of what he had been about to do, and the novelty of that was almost greater than that of the arousal he felt over the kiss.

Guilt. Guilt and uncontrollable lust. He couldn't remember when he had felt either thing.

It was a heady cocktail, and one that did nothing to dampen the desire that he felt.

He wanted to luxuriate in that shame.

Because there was something about it that made him feel…human.

It had been a very long time since he had felt human.

"Enough," he said, setting her back away from him.

"Why?" she asked, her eyes wide, her breathing fast and hard. "Why is it enough? It seems as if it is very clearly not enough."

"Annick," he said. "This was a dancing lesson, nothing more."

"I don't want just dancing. Show me this."

"No," he said, his voice hard, rough. A stranger's voice.

He was choked on his need for her, and he felt nearly dizzy with it. She was…

She was practically glowing, like a magical creature the likes of which he did not believe really existed.

But then, anyone who could make him feel…anything on par with what he did now was… Something he had not expected.

"I wish to know myself. You said that I should. How can I know myself if I don't know what it is to be a woman?"

"When you choose a man to teach you," he said, his voice rough, "he will be one who can give you what you want. Who can be gentle with you. To be slow and teach you all the things your body can do."

"Are you saying you could not?"

"I could do things to you that would make you scream. I can make you forget your name. But I'm not gentle. And I'm not patient. I'm not the kind of lover a virgin should have."

"Then I will find a man. And have him dispense of my virginity at once. So that I might have you before you leave. For I find I wish to know what it is to be naked with you."

"The hell you will," he said, the possessive statement coming out of his mouth before he could stop it.

"It is…that thing. Catch Thirty-Two."

"Twenty-Two."

"You will not have me if I'm a virgin." She spread her hands. "You do not wish me to go become *not* a virgin."

"You're losing focus. Your virginity has nothing to do with whether or not you're good at running a country."

"I want to *live*," she said. "And until I get past all these confusions, I don't know how I'm going to. How will I be Queen? Tell me this, Maximus King. Because I do not know how to be a person. I was a child, and then I was a prisoner. I became a woman physically while locked in a cell. But I have not learned to dress myself. I have not learned to dance. I have not learned what to do when I feel these things."

"A tip for you," he said. "You enjoy spending time in bed. Make work of exploring your body while you do so. It might help take the edge off."

She stared at him, her eyes owlish. "I would not know where to begin with such an endeavor."

"Annick," he said, his voice rough. "Trust

me when I say you don't want to explore these things with me."

"You are to be my husband, eh? *Your* big idea! So, we will eventually."

"All right, then," he said, forcing his voice into a neutral space, not allowing the red flame of rage he felt at the very idea to take hold. "Take another lover first."

"Why?"

"I told you, you are too innocent."

"Eh. *Innocence.*" She said it like something filthy. "The way that they define innocence. Yes? This… *Virginity.*" She laughed. "As if a man's anatomy is the bringer of knowledge and corruption. *Men.* They think far too highly of themselves. I saw my parents murdered. That is what a man stole from me. I have not been *innocent* for a very long time."

Her words struck at a strange place inside of him, and he found that the real reason he wanted to turn away was not the differences between them, but that common bond.

For he did not wish to discuss that. Not ever. Did not wish to face the darkness inside of them that might just match.

He was more comfortable alone.

For the kind of man he was, it was better. It was the only way.

And he knew full well that it wasn't entirely for her benefit that he turned away. Yes, he needed to protect her. Because there was no point, no point at all in pretending that what he was doing was to keep her safe if he became the one to cause her harm. But there were things that were better left uncovered inside of him. And protecting her came hand in hand with protecting himself. At least, in this instance it did.

She had been made victim enough. She didn't need to be exposed to the demons, to the darkness that she seemed to have the power to unleash inside of him.

There were any number of women who didn't call to that thing, that creature that lived down in the deepest recesses of his fractured soul. But he could feel Annick scraping at the bonds of it.

And he wouldn't do that to either of them.

He wasn't a good man. But he worked at not embracing the monster.

And so, he would walk away now. It was the best thing. It was the only thing.

"When is your coronation?"

"We have a week. And then we will announce our engagement."

"Good."

"What does that mean? Good?"

"We have a goal. We have a plan." He looked her over. "I would thank you not to go off script again."

"Oh," she said. "Are my virginal fumblings too much for you to resist? I can't think why else you would need to warn me away so."

"It's for your own good. Trust me."

A small smile curved her lips. "This is the problem. I do not trust anyone."

And he left with the distinct feeling that he had not succeeded in gaining the upper hand.

He was avoiding her. It was an irritation. Ever since their kiss in the ballroom, he had made himself scarce.

They had conducted lessons of a kind, but often they involved other people. He had brought in a body language expert; he had brought in stylists. And from that point on she had been surrounded by women who had spoken to her about being her true self and other things that seemed somewhat ridiculous to her.

None of this was actually about being her true self. It was all strange lies, a rallying cry she could not get her head around.

She did not need to be her true self.

She needed to be a woman who looked like she could be Queen.

It made a mockery of what she wanted, which was actually to know who she truly was. She wanted to understand. Wanted to be something other than a useful tool. She just couldn't see a future where that was possible.

She had hoped. For a grim little while, she had hoped.

And that hope now felt sharp. Made her feel ill-used.

It would have been better to have no hope at all.

Still, she had succeeded in putting together a wardrobe that pleased her. The clothes that she had chosen were exactly as she had told Maximus she wanted them to be. They felt like armor.

The red dress that she would wear tonight on the eve of her coronation had long sleeves, a plunging neckline that revealed a wide V of pale skin. The fabric was stitched into clever panels that looked a bit like individual pieces of armor. It was a thick weighted fabric that held that shape even as she moved. And yet there was something incredibly feminine about it. And it made her feel strong.

She had been paraded around in soft white things for years. Her blond hair loose, as soft as everything else. Barely any makeup.

She looked in the mirror now. At the woman who would be Queen, and she was satisfied that it was a transformation.

Her hair was down, but slicked back, behind her ears and flowing down her back, a golden waterfall. Her lipstick was the same red as the dress, her eye makeup a pale bronze. She looked like she could just as easily lead troops into battle as she could dance the waltz.

And that seemed a triumph in and of itself.

At this event, she would also be introducing Maximus as her fiancé.

And she tried not to curl in on herself with embarrassment over everything that had transpired between them.

It wasn't like she hadn't seen him.

It was just… She wanted him.

And the fact that he was so immune to her…

It was an interesting thing.

Being beholden to such…typical feelings. Embarrassment and jealousy over his past lovers. Insecurity about her own appeal as a woman. She had never worried about that. In fact, she had always hoped that she was not overly appealing as a woman. She didn't want to fend men off. She didn't want to be seen as beautiful. It was a dangerous thing. Just like her softness and her femininity was not something to enjoy.

So, feeling a different relationship to those sensations was…

It was all very strange.

As was the embarrassment.

She looked at herself in the mirror one last time and found that she could not feel embarrassed when she remembered what she looked like. Not tonight.

For tonight, she looked like everything she could hope to be. Strong, a warrior. And beautiful besides. Like something that

Maximus would have to notice. Though she should not care if he did.

She lifted her chin high and walked out into the corridor. And there he was. Looking resplendent in a perfectly fitted suit. He was clean-shaven, his dark hair looking disreputable. As if someone had just run their fingers through it.

No wonder the media wrote such things about him. He always looked like he was both perfectly put together and like he had just exited a lover's bed.

Even she took in those undertones from his appearance, and she could not recall having ever seen a person who had recently left a lover's bed. She had certainly never left one.

"What?" he asked, lifting a brow. "You look angry."

"I'm not."

She frowned even deeper.

"And beautiful."

"Well, thank you," she said, smiling in a way that bared her teeth. "I do not know what I should have done if you, the man who has rejected my advances, did not find me

beautiful. I might curl in on myself and im-
plode into a glorious ash pile of sadness."

"That is quite acidic, even for you."

"Perhaps I feel acidic. But here we are,
ready to make our debut to the world as a
couple. So I suppose we had better look as
if you're not disgusted by my touch."

That flame flickered in his eyes, and she
felt echoing tension inside her in response.

"Who said your touch disgusted me?" he
asked.

"You recoiled from me quickly enough last
week, and besides, you have avoided being
alone with me ever since."

"I'm not here to prop up your self-esteem."

"No, indeed not."

"Which means I should not answer your
provocations," he said.

"Why should you now?" she said darkly.
"You haven't before."

He took hold of her wrist and turned her
to face him. "You should thank God I have
not answered your provocations," he said.
"And that I have kept barriers between us."

"Right. Because you are protecting me?
From the things that I want?"

"From distractions. From harm."

"You forget," she whispered. "You forget what I have been through."

"I don't forget. It's why I won't do anything."

They quit speaking after that. Instead, they walked toward the ballroom, and when they arrived at the door, he took her arm. But no sooner.

Everything that happened after that was a blur. They and their engagement were announced by her right-hand woman, her adviser. And the ripple that went through the room was undeniable.

The stir that they created was unlike anything Annick had ever experienced before, and she found it difficult to separate her response to what was happening around them and to touching him.

Mostly, she was angry. That no matter how she put this armor on, no matter how she worked to ready herself for this, no matter that it was her plan, she still felt...

She still felt like a woman who had been imprisoned for the better part of a decade. A woman who didn't actually know enough about life to understand what she was feeling. And now she had announced her engagement to this man. Announced her intent to make him King.

There was nothing real here, no feeling. No love.

She was always an emblem, never a human. Even in this. In her impending marriage.

She had not given thought to marriage, and then it had seemed as if a marriage to him would be a solution and not a lance of pain in her chest. Not a further bit of recognition that she was only now, and would always be, sad little Annick whose trappings mattered, never her heart.

She would have to make a speech. She was being propelled up to the podium. It was what she had known would happen. She had words prepared, but suddenly she wasn't sure if they would come out right.

"Good evening," she said. "I thank you all for taking the time to come here for my coronation. It is officially a new day for our country. For too long we were kept under the rule of an oppressive regime. And many of you felt as if I may have played a part in it. But over the last year, I hope that what I have done is earn your trust. And now, as I prepare to ascend the throne as Queen, I offer you this assurance. That I have chosen a King, who will rule as Kings have done here for centuries. Maximus King is just the sort of modern man you can trust as your ruler. He will be fair. I will carry out the legacy of my family, not ruling in the same way as my father, but hopefully realizing the progress that would have been made had things gone as they should have. And I will have Maximus, and his influence and strength to guide Aillette. He will bring with him the modern sensibility that many of you would like to see enacted here. While providing the traditionalists with the figurehead they wish to see. He will also bring business acumen. And we have been in discussions for how to increase industry here and strengthen the reserves of this country, and the riches of its people. It is a new dawn for us. A new day. And I am happy to ascend the throne as Queen Annick, with King Maximus by my side."

She nodded, and the room erupted into applause. Maximus stood beside her, tall and strong, and saying nothing. And for once, it felt like her plan had worked.

It was just that inside she still felt a little bit broken. A little bit lost. Uncertain about what to do. But he was there, and he was steady. And nothing about him seemed uncertain at all. And so there was that. There was that. Which was a great blessing.

She didn't understand herself. That she was irritated that he provided her with the strength that she had wanted him to provide her with. That the people had reacted to him with such great satisfaction. Which proved that he was what she needed all along. But she'd known that. Why should she be upset about it?

Because somewhere deep down she had hoped she would be enough, she supposed.

Because what she had begun to tell him days ago was that part of her had hoped that she could overcome her people's doubts by being a woman who led with her heart. Who found a level of honesty with her people that those before her had not.

Because she wanted to be different, and

she realized that, given the circumstances, she had to be the same.

That she could find a balance, find some progress, but she wouldn't be able to be fully her own person, not really.

Because things were too tentative. And it was more important she looked solid than that she be loved.

And it was the source of her dissatisfaction now.

Ridiculous.

But then, she felt slightly ridiculous.

To care so deeply about this now, when she'd been handed what she needed to be protected. When he was living no more authentically than she.

He was helping her. Shouldn't that be enough?

"Shall we dance?"

And she didn't have a chance to respond. And truly, there was no response to make other than yes. For he was now her fiancé in public, even if he was still her adversary in private.

And there was nothing she could do about

it. It was a scheme of her own making, a plan she had seen as a necessity.

You have to see it through. Your feelings don't matter.

Her feelings never mattered.

There was no use becoming morose about it now.

He took her in his arms, and she found herself returning to that floating sensation. That strange place where she was caught between memory, dreams and reality. Suspended between all three.

And held fast only by him.

She felt unbearably fragile in that moment when she should've felt strong.

She was doing it. Her plan was working. And yet she felt reduced.

Yet she felt...

And she could see it, hear an old song rising up inside of her. One that she tried not to remember.

Her father's soft voice singing as he danced her around the ballroom.

When the memories started, she could not stop them. No matter how hard she tried.

CHAPTER NINE

SHE PULLED HERSELF free of his arms. "I must excuse myself," she said, smiling, because people were watching. The whole gilded, glittering ballroom was filled with people, like it had not been since she was a girl. And tomorrow, she would be crowned Queen. And all of it was simply too much.

She remembered this room full of her family.

And they weren't here.

She remembered dancing now. Dancing with her father.

As she never would again.

"Excuse me," she said again, and took as many dignified steps out of the ballroom as she could manage. Before she started to run. To flee out into the garden, praying that the night sky that enveloped her now would simply swallow her whole. Open up and pull her into the black velvet, cover her with the diamond stars. Conceal her. Conceal this weakness from her people. Even from herself.

She had thought, given a year of time away from everything, that she would be stronger. That she would be braver. That she would be prepared to cope with all of this, but instead, the changes that were being instigated around her only reminded her of everything she'd lost. She did not feel a whole year advanced from her captivity. Rather, she felt like she had been brought back to the stage when she had been taken. When her world had been shattered.

She ran down the garden path until she saw a stone bench. Then she flung herself over the bench, curling around the stone and weeping.

She never wept.

Queen Annick of Aillette could not afford to show such weakness.

And so she'd hidden it. Hidden it because what other choice did she have?

And then she felt strong, warm hands on her waist, lifting her up off the ground, pulling her from the depths of her misery. And she fought. Like a hissing, spitting cat, because how dare he? She was angry. And she was upset. Devastated. And half of it was his fault. She did not deserve to be pulled out of her darkness. Rather, she wanted to pull him down into it.

And so she fought him. Until he grabbed her wrists, steadying her, pinning her against his chest. He moved her arms down, fixing them low at her back, her breasts brought up against the wall of his chest.

"What the hell are you doing?"

"I hate you," she said, seeing him suddenly as the emblem of everything that was bad. "I don't feel strong. This was supposed to make me strong. I feel a failure. That I need you to stand beside me to keep me safe. That I am not enough. That I do not magically know everything, that I cannot stand on my own strength because it is not there. That I feel alone in a ballroom full of people, where the ghosts feel more real than those who actually stand next to me. I feel like a twelve-year-old girl who was shut away, locked in time, and yet I know I am not a girl. Because a girl would not want the things that I do. With you. I cannot even have that. I cannot lead my country without you, and I cannot stand to be with you."

"I am an enemy of your own making, Annick," he said, his voice rough. "Your anger with me is not my fault."

"It is," she hissed, wiggling against him. "You were supposed to help. You were supposed to help, and instead you've made me even more confused. And you make me feel all these things. Me, I do not like it."

She could feel her grasp on her English slipping as emotion rose inside of her. "This was supposed to be a special night for me, and it is nothing. Nothing but... Nothing but a reminder. It is all wrong."

"Do you know what this is?"

"What?"

"Grief," he said, his voice a fractured pane of glass. "It's grief. You've been locked away for so long that you never got to have it. You had to protect yourself. You had to save yourself. But all those memories that you put away are out here. And believe me, I get it."

"Why? Because you too have grief?"

"Yes. And because I too have been running from it."

He stared at her, his eyes burning into hers. And that flame wasn't banked. Wasn't low or subtle now. Was more than a flicker.

It was an inferno.

"Then what do we do? How do we keep running?"

"I know," he said, his thumb dragging along her lower lip. "I know just how to keep it away."

"Please," she whispered.

And then he was kissing her, her wrists still pinned against her lower back, caught in one of his large hands, as he tasted her with a ferocity that shocked her.

He had been so adamant that they could not. So adamant that it was bad, and now, he was kissing her with an immediacy that made a complete mockery of everything he'd said before.

"Why?" she whispered, in the brief moment when their lips parted, so that they could both draw breath.

"Maybe because I am a monster," he said. "And maybe you are too. My darkness sees yours. And I cannot resist it."

Her heart pounded faster, harder. Because that at least seemed true.

All the rest of this, all the rest was a farce. Playing a game so that the people of her country would accept her. Playing a game so that she would look strong while she felt like she was breaking apart. Allowing him to assume some kind of control when she didn't want him to have any. But she also wanted him. And there was an honesty to that.

She had no expectations of what things between men and women were like. Though the way that the women who worked for her spoke of it, she did not know if it was commonly such a dark and terrifying thing. A monster all of its own.

But she wasn't like them.

She wasn't like anyone.

She'd known that for years. Lying in her dungeon room, she'd known it. There weren't a lot of other girls who had spent their formative years like she had. It had made her feel terribly lonely to realize that. Made her feel very alone.

Except, looking at him, she realized that he wasn't like anyone either.

This man who was capable of being so charming. Who was so beautiful, but at the same time so very deadly.

Who was brilliant and charming, and also dark and terrifying.

Who could give pleasure with his hands, and take life with them too.

He was like no one. And neither was she.

And in that singularity, they met.

In their darkness, there was a bond.

And so they didn't speak again. She simply kissed him. Learning the movements. Learning the way that his tongue felt best sliding against hers. Learning to glory in the strength of his hold.

Learning to love the way she was delicate, the way he was strong. She had never in her wildest dreams thought that she would like that.

In fact, when she had first begun to fantasize about finding a lover, she had imagined that she might like one she felt most easily in control of, but from the beginning she had been enticed by Maximus's strength. By the danger in him.

What she really wondered was if she would

ever truly be aroused if she did not feel she was overcome.

Because there was some strange and wicked strength to be found in this. In the fact that she seemed strong even while he had her arms trapped.

Because she could see that he had been pushed to the edge. That he was pushed to his limits. That in many ways, she had control over him.

It was a magical thing. Mystical and quite beyond her understanding. So she didn't try to understand.

She simply kissed him. Simply reveled in the deep desire that coursed through her body as his tongue played games with hers.

As her heart tried to beat its way out of her chest.

She struggled, her breasts rubbing against the hard wall of muscle that had her trapped there. And a pulse throbbed between her legs.

Oh, how she wanted him.

She was mindless with it.

And this felt right. In this sea of confusion, amid all the things she didn't know, she knew this.

That she was a woman, and he was a man. And this was everything that was good about those facts. This desire, this need and the sparks that it created between them, with everything wonderful about what it meant.

And the idea that she might be closer to knowing one more thing about herself, to finding a sense of completion, gave her peace even in this storm.

And so she kissed him.

Finally, finally, he released his hold on her wrists, and she was free. She moved her hands to his face, to his shoulders, down the front of his chest. She grabbed hold of his tie and began to loosen the knot with clumsy fingers. She had no idea about the mechanics of a man's tie. Did not have a clue how to begin undressing him, only that she wanted him undressed.

He might not be her true King. But here, now, she wanted him to have this dominion over her body.

Here and now, in the middle of all the lies,

this was real. It was true. There was no one here to see. It was not a show.

It was just her. And him.

And there were very few moments in her life that had this kind of honesty. If any.

And this was what she needed. Something real to hold on to. Something that felt good and not just sad. Not just like a tragedy that left a yawning, darkened void behind.

Maximus was creating a need inside of her, while the sweep of his hands over her body was answering that need.

He was making her want, but he wasn't leaving her wanting. And it was magical to discover these sensations.

He had told her to go to her room and explore her own body, and she hadn't even tried. It wasn't her own touch she wanted. It was his.

She wouldn't have known where to begin. Because she wanted what he was doing. And she was so ignorant she didn't even know how to fantasize about it. But this...

This was it.

And it wasn't all fairy dust and gossamer. There was an edge to it. Like the black velvet of the night sky had wrapped itself around them, cloaking them in darkness. A soft, brilliant darkness that enticed them both to sin.

That enticed them both to satisfaction.

She got that tie free and began to undo the buttons on his shirt.

Oh, she wished she could see better. Because his chest felt magnificent.

And she felt insatiable.

"What is this?" she asked, panting heavily. "I don't know if I want to lick you or bite you."

"Do either," he said, his voice rough. "Both."

And so she did. She leaned in, and she bit his pectoral muscle, and then she soothed it with the flat of her tongue.

"Is this normal? I am hungry for you." She pressed her face to his body and inhaled deeply. The scent of him only made her that much more aroused. "I think it might be madness."

"It is madness," he said. "And this is why I told you to stay away from me."

"You said you were not insatiable."

"But I looked at you and knew that I could

be. And I don't think even a woman with years of experience can handle me insatiable. I should not be asking you to."

"But I need it," she said, tears gathering in her eyes. "I need something strong enough to block out the memories. To block out the bad things. I need something strong enough to make me feel good, because there is so much sadness. There is so much. And sometimes I feel like I might be crushed beneath the weight of it. But not when you kiss me. Because whatever this feeling is that you create inside of me, it is enough. It is strong enough... It is strong enough to make it feel good."

Because the pain was still there. The weight was still there. And this was not a light trip through a field of daisies. But it created in her pleasure at an intensity that matched the difficult things, and if that wasn't a gift, she didn't know what was.

She moved back to him, burying her face in the curve of his neck and kissing him. Licking him.

This was real.

The whole facade of the marriage, of the

two of them together, might be for show, but this was not.

She was so very hungry for real.

More even than pastries.

"Don't hold back," she said.

Because she had a feeling he would try. She had a feeling he would try, and she didn't want him to. Didn't want him to be able to.

She wanted him to be as lost as she was. Utterly and completely, in the madness of this sensual haze. In this dark intensity of need.

She pushed his shirt and jacket from his body, leaving him naked from the waist up. The moonlight shone over his muscles, and she could see that he was indeed a weapon. A lethal, masculine weapon filled with great and terrible beauty. It was exactly the sort of beauty that she coveted. For it was frightening and made her heart stutter, but it also made her feel strong. Safe.

And she was a warrior woman in a red dress made of armor, and whatever they were about to do, the battle they were about to engage in, the war for pleasure, she knew they were both going to be well able to withstand it.

She unzipped her gown, let it fall down to the floor, and suddenly she felt vulnerable. Standing out there naked in the moonlight. Wearing nothing more than a pair of red lace panties that scarcely covered anything.

She was bare to him.

His hands moved to his belt, to the closure on his slacks, and he took the rest of his clothes off. Even in the dim light, she could see that he was thick and strong, larger than she had imagined a man might be there. But it also thrilled her. Because she was not afraid of this. She had withstood a great many things. Had endured atrocities she had not wished to endure. And this was her choice.

A great mystery of life that had not been taken from her forcibly, something she had always been grateful for. And she was choosing it. Here with this man who made her wild with desire. Who made her feel something better than normal.

And then that big, warrior man knelt down before her, and she found his strong arms wrapping themselves around her waist and lowering her slowly to the stone bench as he leaned in, pressing his mouth against the needy heart of her, lapping at her with intensity that gave no quarter to her inexperience. Just as he had warned.

She did not have the time to express shock. She could only hold tightly to his head as he feasted upon her. As the aggressive strokes of his tongue pushed her to that promised place that had been created in her with the touch of his lips to hers.

Then he pushed a finger deep inside of her, stroking at her core, at a place inside of her that incited a riot of need. The invasion was foreign, but wonderful, and when he added a second finger, she gasped. It was too much, but it couldn't be. For if she hoped to have that most masculine part of him inside of her, she would have to get used to this.

And quickly, she did. Quickly, the intrusion, the friction, became welcome, as he lapped at her more firmly with his tongue.

And then little ripples began to spread inside of her. Her need growing, opening up. Expanding, until she was made almost entirely of it. Until she thought she might die of it.

And then he sucked that sensitized bundle of nerves into his mouth, the suction making her crazy. Causing her pleasure to break over her like a wave. She cried out, her legs draped over his shoulders, her heels digging into his back. And she didn't care if anyone heard. She cared about nothing. Nothing but this.

And then he was there. She was still seated on the edge of the bench, the thick head of his arousal pressing against her. He gripped her behind and impaled her with his length, and she gasped, the searing pain she felt a shock, particularly on the heels of such great pleasure.

But he didn't stop.

He thrust into her like a mad animal, his teeth scraping against her collarbone.

And somewhere, in the pain and uncertainty, a thread of pleasure began to wrap itself around both, binding them up. Until she couldn't tell which was which. Until she couldn't make out what was him, what was her. What was pain, what was need. Until they were both made of stars. And she could tell when he reached the edge, when he began to shatter as she had done. "Come for me," he growled, and just like that, she did. Just like that, she broke again.

Only a moment before she had been consumed by the amount of unknowns in the world. By how adrift she felt. By how not her she was.

But lying there, sprawled indecently in the darkness of the garden with Maximus inside of her, she felt like she had an answer.

She did not know what it was for.

But as she held on to him, she felt rooted to the earth.

Grounded in a way she could not remember ever feeling before. And it was…a revelation.

"I'm sorry," he said, gruff as he removed himself from her.

"Don't," she said, feeling like she was made of spun glass. Not sure if she loved or hated it. "Don't apologize."

"Why not?" he asked, his shoulders tight, his whole body gone stiff like a stone.

"I don't want you to. I don't want you to apologize. It was wonderful."

He looked away, his face shrouded in shadow. "I was rough with you. I hurt you."

"Life has hurt me worse than you ever could. At least you made pleasure out of the pain. I did not know such a thing was possible. And there, I have learned a lesson."

"Don't," he bit out. "Don't excuse me."

"Me, I am not forgiving," she said. "If I wished to be angry at you I would be. But I wanted this. Choice is one of the most beautiful things in this world," she said. "It is our own choices that spin together the being that we are, and I have had so many years of choice being taken from me. And the position I find myself in now, one where I must be a good Queen. One where I must protect myself… My enemies still take choices from me, Maximus. Back me into corners where only one option remains. To fight as I can. It is why I took you. It is why I agreed to this marriage. But this…*this* I chose. Do not take this from me too. I wanted to know. I… Sometimes I feel crushed beneath the weight of the things I don't know, but at least I know this. At least I chose this."

"You don't understand," he said. "I was close to being out of control and…"

"And what?"

"I can't afford to lose myself. There is a darkness in me that I keep on a leash."

"And you only let it out to play when you take a job that allows it? When you decide that you are engaging in a quest for vengeance? Is that it?"

"You can't possibly understand," he said.

"Alors!" She made a face of mock horror. "Of course I cannot. I'm just a virgin. And you know so much more than me."

"We must go back to the ball."

He dressed her, the movements perfunctory, and she felt herself beginning to crack. But she would not allow him to see. "There are some things you are going to have to trust me about," he said.

She stared at him, trying to figure this man out. What he wanted. Why he seemed so filled with regret. He was supposed to be a playboy who had sex as easily as most people breathed. And this was not easy.

She did not like it.

"Yes, I will allow for that when it comes to you teaching me how to look strong. But I will not allow for that when it comes to you teaching me what my body wants. When it comes to teaching me what my heart wants. If that was darkness, then I want more of it. For, me, I am a little bit dark myself." She tried to smile.

He was dressing, and he didn't look at her. So, her show of bravado didn't seem to matter.

"I can't love you," he said.

She jerked back. "No one loves me," she said. "Why should you matter?"

He looked like she'd struck him with her words. But they were a truth. Why should she know them and he be spared them?

"No one?" he asked.

"No. My family are dead. My people… They certainly don't love me. Look at the great lengths I'm having to go to in order to be accepted. And then there is my staff. They have become friends of a sort. But it is not love. No one loves me. It is no matter to me if you are added to the great list of those on this earth who do not."

"It's not…"

"People love you, though, don't they? Your sisters. Your mother and father. Your friend Dante. Yes, I have done research on all those in your life. He loves you too. He's like a brother. Is he not?"

"Well, yes," Maximus said. "Though him sleeping with my sister has complicated some things."

"He married your sister."

"Semantics."

She tilted her head to the side. "You are an image maker—aren't semantics your business?"

"To an extent," he said.

She swallowed hard, a sense of unfairness building inside her she could not quite come to grips with. Of course she didn't want him to be unloved. But he did not seem to know how to accept love, and she would very much like some love. "How very good it must be to be loved by so many. Do they know…do they know how dark you are inside?"

"No," he said. "And I would do just about anything to keep the truth from them."

"It would hurt them."

"Yes."

This honesty was rare for him, she knew. And as gifts went, a small one she would take. An intimacy that somehow felt deeper than what they'd shared with their bodies. Though perhaps one had led to the other. Stripped barriers away that might otherwise have stood.

"Why don't you tell them?"

He paused for a long moment. "There are some things you don't want to burden other people with."

"I see." She looked at him and recognized at that moment the weight he carried. It was not unlike hers. Not so different. "You can burden me. For I do not love you either. You do not love me. That is simple, eh? We help each other."

"You've been through enough."

"Yes. Just enough to be strong. To be strong enough that even when you hurt me it does not hurt so much."

She found that she liked much better being

trusted to take the strength of his darkness, the strength of his need, than being told she was too weak when she had endured so much and had stayed standing. When she had endured the kinds of things that would have reduced lesser people to rubble.

She would rather stand here with him. Her body buzzing, throbbing, feeling fragile and strong all at once. Like the thinnest of unbreakable glass.

"Let us go," he said, offering her his arm.

"You're going to leave me alone tonight, aren't you? You're not going to listen."

"You were a virgin," he said, his voice rough. "Surely even you can see that you might need a little bit of time to recover."

She would have laughed if she hadn't felt so fragile. Something as big as a laugh might make her crumble. "Life has never given me a moment to recover."

"Then consider it the first sensitive thing life has done for you."

"Eh." She waved her hand. "Nobody wants a sensitive penis, Maximus. One prefers them hard."

"You talk a big game for a woman who has seen precisely one."

"A good one, I think."

"Annick…"

She saw this moment then, for what it was. He was acting as if she was the innocent, the one who needed protection.

But for whatever reason, it was her soldier who needed this. Who needed this distance.

"Fine. I will let you play the part of gentleman tonight. But only because *you* need to. *I* do not need you to. But if you need to feel good, if you need to feel redeemed for what you have done to me, then I allow it. But tomorrow…tomorrow is my coronation. And you must stand up with me. And then tomorrow night… I will be a Queen. And don't you think then I might be strong enough for you?"

"Remember what this is."

She lifted a shoulder. "There is no name for what this is. You cannot play the part of a more experienced man. Not now. Not with this. We are both virgins in this, I think."

She walked on ahead of him, and she knew that her hair might look mussed, that she might not look the perfectly put together warrior woman she had looked when she had first gone into the ballroom tonight. But she felt stronger. Somehow, now, she felt that the armor was underneath her skin, rather than just draped over her body in red fabric.

And there was something to be said for that.

For laying claim to at least one of the mysteries in the universe.

Yes, there was something to be said for that as well.

And even if she still felt raw, and a little bit vulnerable, she also felt strong.

And she would happily take that and lay claim to it.

CHAPTER TEN

"WHAT EXACTLY IS going on?"

Maximus was the unhappy recipient the next morning of a group video call from both of his sisters, and his friend Dante, who was also now his brother-in-law.

He was rocked by the previous night. By his encounter with Annick, and even more so by the conversation after.

I will let you play the part of gentleman tonight. But only because you need to.

He was a man who lived a life in the shadows, and Annick seemed to have the ability to drag him into the light.

If you need to feel redeemed for what you have done to me...

Oh, Annick. If only she knew, there was no redemption, not for a man like him.

"Obviously my engagement has been announced?" he said, shutting his thoughts down and grinning into the screen, as was expected of him.

"Your engagement. To the Princess of a principality that until very recently was run by a crazed despot," his friend Dante said.

"Yes. The very one."

"How did that...?" It was Violet who asked that question, though she wasn't able to finish it. She was staring into the camera, looking comically confused.

"How these things normally work, Violet," he said, as if his sister was terribly slow. "Kidnap."

"Kidnap," she said. "You're not telling me that tiny little creature kidnapped you. That's embarrassing. At least *I* was kidnapped by a very large man."

She reclined in her chair, round with her pregnancy and looking amusingly embarrassed on his behalf.

"Don't underestimate a small woman with a large amount of determination, Violet," he said. "I've decided to go ahead and allow the kidnap. Just as I decided to go ahead and pursue an engagement with my beautiful captor. Why wouldn't I?" He affected the most charming smile he could. "Think of all the things I've done. There isn't a very long list of things I haven't. Virgin Princesses? Well, that was a stone left unturned. And the opportunity to be King? She's being crowned Queen today. And in Aillette that makes me King."

"Seems unearned," Violet said.

"And strange," Dante added.

"But you should at least admire her industriousness in procuring herself the husband she wanted. She chloroformed me."

"Did she?" Minerva looked positively delighted by this news.

"Of course you would like it," Dante said. "Given you ended up engaged to me because of a rather grand lie you told on TV. It was very nearly kidnap."

"I *did* do that," Minerva said. "I really do admire women who go after what they want. If I would've thought of chloroform, I would've used that."

"And to think," Dante said, addressing Maximus. "You worried about your sister when I married her. You should've been worried for me."

"Don't worry about me," Maximus said. "Everything is well in hand. You can tell Dad and Mom that they can come visit the palace sometime."

"Well, Mom will like that," Violet said. "Two children married into royalty. And you only married a billionaire, Minerva. You look like the slouch out of the group."

Minerva did look angry about that, since she historically felt left behind. "But I gave them their first grandchild," she said.

Regret kicked against his stomach. Because he had not used birth control with Annick last night. And though children between them was somewhat inevitable, she was young and it did not have to be now. He did his best to push the thought aside. What was done was done. He had a feeling there would be no asking Annick to procure any sort of emergency contraceptives. He could only imagine the scathing that would earn him. She would do precisely what she pleased and nothing else. That much he knew.

"You will all be invited to the wedding, of course." To do anything else would be strange. He was almost troubled by how easily he lied to his family. But he'd been doing it for so many years that it was second nature. Second nature to smile like this, to make jokes about how he was doing this simply to enrich the portfolio of all that he'd done. Yes, this kind of subterfuge was easy. He didn't even feel guilty about it.

No, what he felt guilty about was taking Annick's virginity. A novelty within a novelty. He had been...rough. He should not have taken her on a stone bench without a care for the pain she might've experienced. But he had.

He thought back to what she'd said.

You need this...

He pushed it aside. He didn't *need* anything. And he didn't need to have her again.

Control was his.

He would not give in to the beast inside of him.

To do otherwise made him no different than the men he took out of this world. The men he hated above all else.

If he could not protect her, then his life was forfeit.

And so, today he would go to her coronation, and tonight, he would reinstitute the distance between them.

There really was nothing else to be done.

She was to be Queen today.

Annick looked in the mirror at her sleek reflection. Her hair was piled up atop her head, ready for a crown. For coronation. She wondered what it would have been like if life had gone the way it was supposed to.

Her parents would still be dead. That was the nature of coronations. It was why they were, in her opinion, sort of a terribly barbarous thing. A ceremony. Passing the torch. But only when the flame of your loved one was extinguished.

And Annick... Well, she never should've been Queen.

She squeezed her eyes shut and tried her best not to think of Marcus, her older brother. The one who should have been standing here today. The one who should have always been here.

And then she tried not to think of Maximus. Of the way her body burned when she remembered what had transpired between them last night.

This day was to be a ceremony, celebrating her becoming Queen. A coronation. Essentially, she was being recognized as a woman. At the moment, it all felt a bit too literal. For last night, she had been introduced to another dimension of what it meant to be a woman. For last night, she had…

And he had turned away from her.

She had never felt half so alone as she did going back into that ballroom without him. As she did for the whole rest of the evening, in a space filled with hundreds of people.

She had given a good speech, had found a strength in herself that she had not known was there, but it had done nothing to ease the loneliness in her.

She was good at standing alone.

But she was tired of it.

And she had not yet seen him today.

Today she was wearing emerald green. A brocade fabric made up the gown, which was shaped like a large bell, the fabric making dramatic folds, billowing out around her feet.

The door to her chamber opened, and there

he was. He looked stern and striking in a black suit with a black shirt and tie. He looked... Well, he looked like the King. Of her country. And of death.

He looked every inch the assassin that he was.

How did other people not see this? How did they see him and think that he was nothing more than a feckless playboy? It was so patently untrue. So clearly not all he was. Not even remotely.

"The guard has been vetted, checked over and completely cleared. The perimeter is secure. You have nothing to worry about tonight, Annick. I have seen it is safe."

"Well. You had better," she said, keeping her eyes on her own reflection, only glancing at him in the mirror. "It is, after all, why you are here."

"Yes. It is."

"To do anything else would be an abject failure. Are you a failure, Maximus?"

"I think you know that I'm not." He straightened the cuffs on his sleeves, the movement inescapably catching her eye. She looked away as quickly as possible.

"You will escort me to the front of the room for the ceremony today. And when the country pledges their allegiance to me, you will also."

"Will I?"

"Yes," she said. "You know you cannot be King of this country and not be a citizen thereof."

"And is a King beneath his Queen here?"

That brought to mind images of his strong, hard body beneath hers. All that power trapped between her thighs. And in her image, he looked up at her, his eyes fierce, and she knew that to imagine that she might be in control if she were on top was a fiction.

She blinked, ignoring the scorching heat in her cheeks.

"I believe you know he's not," she said, feeling particularly scabby. "But that does not mean I must submit to your nonsense."

"I would never ask you to submit to such a thing."

"Why did you leave me?"

Why could she not keep these sorts of questions inside? Why was she incapable of holding her tongue around him?

It was the strangest thing, for with him she found the core of what she claimed to want: a space where she could be wholly herself.

It was just she could not seem to entirely control it. And that was... Well, that was a double-edged sword.

What they had was nothing more than a mercenary arrangement. He was only able to be King because he would be married to her. And she needed his protection. She would've had to marry someday anyway, so it had been the smartest thing to agree to his demand. Of course it had been. To do anything else would've been stupid. He was the one securing her forces. He was the one making sure she was safe.

Any other man would have far too much power and she would have to be certain she could trust him. There was no reason not to marry Maximus. And there was no reason to be soft and tender about what had occurred between them in the garden. It would have happened eventually. An inevitability. And yet she felt soft and tender, and it didn't matter if it was inevitable.

She wanted to rest her head against his chest.

You are a fool, Annick. You never went soft in all your years of captivity, and now you wish to snuggle up against this hunk of stone?

"I left because it was the best thing to do," he said. "You asked me here to protect you, not to defile you."

"Did we not agree that defiling would happen at a certain point?"

"I believe I told you to take another lover first."

"And what about what I wanted? I didn't want another lover."

"You said that you suspected you were a glutton. That you might wish to make love to any number of men in your lifetime. Why should you settle for having me first?"

"I wanted you. Why should I do anything but have what I want? If I want a pastry for dinner, why should I not have it? If I want you as a lover, why should I not have you?"

"I was not able to be as gentle with you as I should've been."

"I did not ask for gentle," she said. "The

world has not been gentle with me, Maximus King. The world has treated me roughly. And here, I find something that I want. Your body and your mind. Why should I not have this? Because you say so? Because you think you know me? You do not know me. You do not know me any more than I know you. Sharing pastries before dinner together and speaking of sex and gluttony is not knowing me. You do not get to decide how strong I am."

"I would never seek to make decisions about what you can handle. But you don't know me. And you know nothing of sex."

"I know some of it now. That men are hard. And that it hurts when you are inside at first. But then it feels wonderful."

"It won't hurt every time."

"How can it not? You are so very vast."

His lips twitched. "You have a way with words."

"I say it as it is," she said. "And I know my mind."

"We can help each other."

"Can we? Tell me how we can. And tell me why sex would get in the way."

"It's because of me. I need control. Especially on a day like today. I am helping you. *Protecting* you. Keeping you safe. I can't afford to be distracted."

"And why? I feel I have a right to know. What is this distraction you feel you might face? For I have never seen you distracted."

"In the garden last night, an assassin could've come upon us and I would never have known." He touched her chin then, his hands rough. "Until an assassin's bullet pierced your skin."

She shivered. But not with fear.

It was desire, but then… It was a deep, searing pain as she looked into his eyes and saw the echo of old demons there.

This was not a fear rooted in the abstract. He was afraid. He was angry, at himself.

"But he did not," she said, her tone gentle.

"It could've happened. I let my guard down once, and the consequences were severe."

"Tell me." This was the loss he'd suffered. She knew well that he had.

"This is not a topic of discussion open between us," he said.

"Why?"

"Don't test me."

And like that it was over.

He resisted this honesty between them and she could not help it.

He extended his arm, and she took it and he led her out of the chamber.

"Why? I'm not a prisoner anymore. This is not a dungeon, and you are not a dictator. You don't get to tell me what I'm curious about."

"And it is my life. I don't have to share it with you if I don't want to. You are the reason I'm here. You brought us together. You presented a case that was so compelling I couldn't turn away from you. And I have found ways that you could be of use to me. That this *arrangement* could be of use to me. I'm tired," he said, his eyes nearly black now, "of going on missions, of trying to rid the world of evil, one man at a time. It is… It is a dark pursuit. On that you can trust me. If I had a soul, it was shed somewhere along that road in the past fifteen years. And I have not seen it since."

"Then why bother to help me at all? Why bother to try and rid the world of terrible men? If you do not care, if you have no soul inside of your chest, then why are you here at all?"

"Because there was a woman," he said, the words immediately sending a chill through her body. "And she did have a soul. A lovely one. More beautiful than you could imagine. And when she died, I vowed that I would do something about the injustice in the world. Because if I did, then…more people like her would not die."

"Who was she?"

"It doesn't matter. Now you know. Now you understand."

That was not understanding, and his skeleton of a story was not telling. She was reeling, trying to piece the details together, but too soon they arrived at the small chapel where her coronation would be held.

And she had to push aside all thoughts that were not about this moment.

It was a smaller gathering than at the ball last night. Nobility and dignitaries from the country, who had been driven underground during the previous regime, were all there and resplendent in their finery. There were leaders from around the world and a select group of citizens who had been chosen to attend.

It was wonderful. A look at her country in the best light possible. Free and happy and ready to move into the future.

She suddenly felt small and unequal to the task. And as much as it angered her, she was glad that Maximus was there beside her. She was glad that she wasn't doing this alone. Glad that he had offered to marry her, even if she should be appalled to have considered such a thing. Even if she should be angry that she felt she needed a man to assist with her ascension to the throne.

It's nothing to do with being a woman. Or him being a man. And everything to do with spending so much of your life locked in a dungeon...

Yes. She had.

Hadn't Maximus begun teaching her new things? And that made her feel too raw. She couldn't think about that. Not at the moment. She could only focus on putting one foot in front of the other. Could only focus on the solidity of his strength to her right.

It was nearly like a wedding. They walked up the aisle together, but then he left. For it was not him she would be making vows to, not today. It was her country. Her people.

While the priest handed her a scepter, and a robe was draped over her shoulders, she stood. A blessing was spoken over her, and then she spoke the words of affirmation back, vows promising stability. To honor the people, the country, its traditions. To make progress where it needed to be made. To protect and support and heal. And she meant the words. Every last one of them. Because she had survived for this. Had lived for her country. And when the heavy, golden crown was placed on her head, she felt it fully. For this was her cause.

Not pastries and finding out whatever it was she preferred best to eat, and not sex in the garden. This.

The responsibility hurt. Making her heart ache.

But nonetheless, she finished the ceremony and looked out at her people.

"With all that I am," she said. "With my life. I will serve." She swallowed hard, and she pressed on, with words from her heart and not words from a rehearsed script.

For she understood, suddenly. That while she might have to present a certain front, it was her core, who she truly was, that had brought her to this moment.

That had helped her to survive, and to keep her spirit through those long years of captivity.

That had driven her to seek help from Maximus.

Yes, in some cases her choices had felt forced upon her by those who sought to harm her. But it was her strength that allowed her to withstand them.

Not just anyone would have chosen to fly across the world, find the super soldier who had led the mission against her country's dictator, chloroformed him and forced him back to her country.

Not just anyone could stand here in this moment, after being a prisoner. After withstanding an assassination attempt only a month earlier.

Only her.

Queen Annick.

"We lost much when we lost my parents. You lost a King, and with the death of my brother, the future King. And I know that I, as Queen, am an unknown. But with all the strength I possess, I will lead you. I will honor my father, but we will also push forward. This is a new era. We will not hide here in the mountains, a kingdom isolated. We will embrace technology, connecting with the world as we haven't done before. We will grow in strength. Not me, not Annick. But all of us. This strength will not be to subdue, but to stand on our own. All of us. Together."

And then it was done.

"And here now is presented to you," the priest said, "Queen Annick Lestrade of Aillette."

She was met with applause, and she nodded serenely, walking back out of the chapel with Maximus meeting her at the door.

There would be a large luncheon after, tables set up in the gardens outside, but she was not sure she could stomach any food. Or being in the gardens. Considering what had happened the last time she was there.

No. She would be strong. She would not trip at this first hurdle that was not even a hurdle.

And so she spent the rest of the day smiling and speaking to whomever wished to speak to her. By the end of it all she felt every inch the symbol. As if there was nothing of the woman left at all. It was an odd sensation.

And then she looked back at Maximus, and she felt… That she couldn't breathe.

She wanted him. She wanted him again. And it didn't matter that he had been unkind to her. Didn't matter that he had abandoned her. That he had said it was for the best. That he had made it plain that he was not going to share with her or be intimate with her again because of…control. Or whatever else he'd spoken of.

What did you survive the dungeon for?

Wasn't *she* enough of a reason?

Finding this core of herself, recognizing it, made her ask new questions even now.

Did their arrangement have to be solely for her country?

Oh, she cared about it a great deal. She would serve her country, give her life for it. It was true. But couldn't she also want something for herself? Couldn't she have also lived…simply to live? To be touched by a man. As she had been last night. To be able to get married. To be able to have children. To enjoy dresses and makeup.

To enjoy pastries.

She wanted those things. She did not think that it made her bad or selfish. Yet he was all about control. But he would not tell her why.

Here again, she was to be a figurehead.

His wife, but not for real. He would not share with her. He would not sleep with her, because he'd been undone by what had happened between them. She knew it. She'd seen it. Her honesty was a devastating weapon to him. And she would have to hide herself from him. As he would continue to conceal his own secrets.

It would be far too similar to living that dungeon life she had been in for this many years.

She was sad for it.

When the luncheon finished, and the guests had cleared away, she found that Maximus had vanished as well. She gathered her skirts, lifting them up from the ground, and swept back into the palace, moving down the corridor, heading toward his chamber.

Then she walked in. Without knocking, because why would she? He had come into her room without so much courtesy the morning of their dance lesson.

And she was not disappointed. For he was there, his jacket discarded, his shirt partly open, showing a beautiful slice of his chest. That she had licked. Bit. She wanted more of him. She was just so…hungry.

And she wanted someone to share that with.

"I am a woman," she said.

"Yes," he answered. "You are not a coffeepot. That much is certain."

Perhaps her honesty was her greatest weapon, and why should she shield him from it? He was hurting her with his distance. Why should she protect him?

"I am a woman, and a Queen. I am both. And I had the terrible sensation today as I stood up there before the crowd that I would lose myself as the crown was placed upon my head. I thought to myself…this is why I lived. This is. This coronation. This moment. The opportunity to take care of my people. But then I thought…it is not why I lived. I would have lived if I would've lost the country. I would have lived, and it would've mattered. Does it matter?"

"Of course it does," he said. But his face gave nothing away, and he stood rigid.

Though it was that blankness that spoke volumes, at least as far as she was concerned.

"It does," she said. "It matters that I breathe. It *does* matter."

How she wished she could break down his walls. But maybe the fact that she had broken them was evident here. Maybe she had, and that was why he was so horribly blank. So she pressed on. "I am not a person who died." Tears pushed against her eyes. "My family died. There was nothing to be done. My family died, and it is… True sadness. But I'm not dead. I'm not dead and I am more than a figurehead to be trotted out at the whims of…of those men. Those men who saw me as nothing more than…" She blinked back tears. "I would go days sometimes without seeing the sun. All that time

I spent in a dark dungeon. And they would let me out, only to serve them. And in my heart I thought that if I could survive, then I would fix things. And sometimes it gave me the strength to keep going. But sometimes I just thought of being held again. Being loved. Sometimes I just thought that maybe someday there would be a man who would hold me in his arms. And sometimes that was enough."

She waited. She waited, but he did not surprise her. Instead, he did what she'd feared.

"I'm not that man," he said.

"I don't need you to be," she said, desperate now and not caring if he knew it. "But I would like for you to be *you*. I would like for you to not hide what you are—*who* you are—from me. When I am the one who has seen you. I am just so very tired. And so…" She reached behind her back and grabbed the zipper tab of her green dress and released it, letting it fall to the floor. And then stared at him. He looked at her, hunger in his dark gaze, and she felt an intense tug of satisfaction. She was wearing nothing but a strapless lace bra and matching panties. And the shoes that she had not bothered to take off.

"I cannot explain," she said. "I can only feel. Feel the desperate weight of that darkness closing in around me. It was so horrible. I was nothing. Nothing. A tool to be used. And that was what decided if I lived or died, and that is what I had to be. And you can see now why it angers me. To have to say the right things, to do the right things. To dress the right way. When I want me to matter. Me. What I want. And it never will. Not out there. Because you're right. I must be appropriate. I must be what my country needs. But I am also a woman. I am not just a Queen. And I want you. Whether you are rough or not. I want you, the real you. The real… Feelings for me."

"I do not have feelings," he said, his voice going pitch-dark.

"I don't have the words," she said, feeling full to the top with frustration. "Learn French if you want good words. I don't have them in English. Or learn my language. Learn my language if you want to hear something better. Only… I am tired of being contained. I am tired of easy. I want *hurt*. Because hurt is better than nothing at all. The gray and darkness and numbness. Do you have any idea? Do you have any idea what it's like to be locked away like that? No, you don't. Because you were raised rich and with freedom."

He moved toward her, and she could feel the crackle of intensity beneath his skin, could feel it barely contained inside of him, fighting to escape. "I know what it is to be trapped," he ground out. "To be trapped inside a darkness that you cannot fight. To be trapped inside something you cannot even see. Don't tell me that I don't understand."

Her frustration boiled over then, because she was standing there, bared in every way, and he was still resisting this and she simply could not. "Then if you understand, fight against it *with me*. *Feel* with me."

"There's no reason," he said, his voice as rough as gravel. "And it benefits no one to care."

"Lies," she whispered, the word choked by emotion. "You care. Whether you want to or not, whether you want it to be about the sainted woman that you speak of or not, you must care about the world."

"Or maybe I'm simply a killer." He took hold of her arm, drew her to him. She responded. Her nipples going tight, her heart thundering harder. She did not fear him. She felt for him. So much, she might burst with it. "Have you ever thought of that? Maybe I'm filled with hate, and *killing* is the only thing that makes that feel better. Maybe I dress it up in missions and assignments and all of those cold clinical words we use to justify government-sanctioned death. What if I like it? What if I care about that more than I care about fighting for justice?"

"It is not true," she said. "Whatever you say, it is not true. Or you would not have offered to be the King here. You would have simply gone about finding a person to assassinate in order to protect me. You would not have allied yourself with me as you did."

He released his hold on her. "Or perhaps you prove your point. Perhaps you prove your point that killing sometimes creates more problems."

"I don't know." She turned from him, pacing away from him. "I don't know about any of this. But tonight…"

She took the crown from the top of her head and placed it on the dresser by the door.

"Can I be Annick? And you be Maximus? Not the King, not the Queen. But just us. As we are. Can we be simply feeling? It doesn't have to be feelings for me. It can be feelings for her. It doesn't have to be anything easy. It can be sharp. It can be painful. But this… Last night. When I bit you. When I tasted you. I am just starving. I am just starving for all that I could have. For all that I have missed."

He didn't say a word. Instead, he stepped forward, grabbing hold of her hips and dragging her up against his body. She could feel his desire there. His hardness. The need that he felt for her, and he could not deny it. No matter how much he might want to. She pushed at his shirt, shoving it from his shoulders and tearing buttons off it as she did. They scattered across the floor, and then his chest was bare. Just as she liked it.

And she found herself dropping down to her knees before him, undoing the belt on his pants and opening them, reaching her hand inside his underwear and revealing that thick length of him that had felt so incredible inside her the night before. And she was ready. Ready for him. Ready for this. She was ready for everything that he might have for her. But first. She wanted this. This moment to luxuriate in the feel of him. The taste of him. She wanted this moment for them. For her. She wanted this moment to simply be.

She leaned in, sliding her tongue along his length.

"Annick," he growled, taking a handful of her hair, and she felt the pins there biting into her scalp.

Does a King submit to his Queen here?
You know that he does not.

And here she was, on her knees, submitting to her King.

Except, it was not so simple. For he was at his end; she could see that. The fierce light in his eyes, the strength with which he held her in his grip. He was beyond himself, and she was... She was powerful. In this moment, on her knees before him, she was everything. Woman. Queen. Submissive. Powerful. In this moment. Finally, she could feel all the light that she had been denied for all of those years. In his strength. His heat. His taste.

She didn't obey him. Rather, she leaned her head forward, pulling against his hold, loving the way the pain dovetailed with the pleasure that pierced her like an arrow between her legs. And she took him in deep. Tasted him, took him in so deep that he touched the back of her throat. And he growled, bucking his hips upward. And she took it. All of it.

"Annick." He said her name, rough and raw and ragged, and it was everything that she needed it to be.

She lost herself then. In pleasuring him.

In this endless circle of need. It filled her. It emptied her. Giving him pleasure gave her her own, and she could not have explained that if she had been asked to. All she knew was that she wanted it. Wanted him.

All she knew was that she was a slave to this. As much as she was the master of it.

And she had come to him across the world, not because she had thought they might find this, simply because she thought they might be able to help.

But this was more than help. And it was more than simply for her. It was something…

A gift.

Annick had spare few gifts in her life.

A spare few.

He jerked her away from him suddenly, and she could see that he was pushed to his limits, his muscle shaking.

"Not like this," he said, his words a fractured example of the control within.

"Why not? You made me shatter that way last night."

"But I want to be in you, my Queen. I wish to feel how tight you are. How wet. I wish for you to come apart in my arms while I shatter against you."

"Yes," she whispered.

And she would. She would.

"Take your clothes off," he ordered.

And she could hear it. That his restraint had slipped its leash.

That she'd gotten her wish.

And now she would pay the price.

Oh, she craved that price.

He freed himself from the rest of his garments while she undid her bra, drew her panties down her legs. While she kicked her shoes off.

"Yes," he said. "There you are. Not a Queen, are you? Just mine."

"Yes," she whispered.

And she did not know why she found such a great comfort in that. In being his. Except he would never take her to a dungeon. He would never lock her away. He wanted to make her feel good.

As long as she belonged to Maximus, she would be safe.

Suddenly, she wanted to weep. Safe.

She could not remember ever feeling safe. *Safe*.

Safe with him. If she was his, that was how it would be. And he could be hers. She could...

And then she couldn't think anymore, because he closed the distance between them and kissed her. Hard and fierce and long. Kissed her until she couldn't think. Until her world was reduced to the way his hard body felt naked against hers. Then he lifted her up and carried her to the bed.

He was over her, those eyes gleaming and

intense. The eyes of a man who had sat there with his finger steady on the trigger, waiting to take a life. Who had done so to save lives. Who claimed he had no conscience and no soul but held her like she mattered.

And he positioned himself at the entrance of her body, and when he thrust into her, she gasped.

For there was no control, no finesse. All the things he'd said he needed were gone. And she reveled in it. Gloried in it.

For this was what she needed.

This. This moment of abandon. Each thrust was so intense it was nearly painful. Pleasure. Pain. Lights flashing across her closed eyes. Every sensation she could possibly have hoped for cascading over her in the moment. Her need building to such heights she didn't know if she could withstand it.

And yet she would. Because she knew what true hell was. Having nothing. Having no one. Feeling nothing.

Not even knowing what to dream for, so you had to dream of what you might do for your country, and nothing else.

For thinking that the only reason you might

matter was to serve the greater good, and not to simply be.

But in his arms, she could be.

In his arms, the years of deprivation, the years of nothing, melted away.

And when she shattered, she was the stars again. Every starry night she hadn't been allowed to see, as the dungeon ceiling had been her view. She became all she had lost.

When it was over, she lay with him. Let him hold her. Until the sounds of their hearts beating quieted. Until she could breathe again.

"No more prisons," she whispered.

"I do not seek to put you in a prison," he said.

"You may not seek to," she said, tracing a finger over his forearm, "but the end result is the same. By denying me... It is the same." She breathed out slowly. "It is not the same. I know it is not. But sometimes I feel full to bursting with these emotions... I don't ever want to go back. To being nothing and feeling nothing. When I saw my parents... My brother."

He tightened his hold on her. "How did you escape?"

She spread her hands. "I didn't escape, eh?"

His lips curved upward. Only barely. "You lived."

"Yes," she agreed. "I lived. They made sure that I saw the executions of my family." She shook her head, sadness building inside of her. "It is the deepest of sorrows. To have lost them that way. To know that everything in my country would change as well. That it was not just I who lost, but everyone. All of Aillette. And I could do nothing to stop it."

"That's why you kept going."

She nodded. "It was easier that way at first. To think only of my people. To think only of the things that they had suffered, because the things that I suffered…"

"Do not tell me what you suffered," he said. "Tell me of how they lived, not how they died."

She was choked with gratitude. For no one had ever asked for that. No one had given her the opportunity to speak of it. She had denied herself the gift of remembering for too long. Because it was easier. Because it felt simpler to focus only on the fact they were gone, rather than remembering how sweet it was when they were there.

"My older brother liked to tease me. He also gave me sweets. Always. When he and my father would travel together, he would always bring me back something nice. To commemorate the other country. A fruit candy, or a chocolate. Pastries. Cakes." She smiled. "Perhaps that is why I liked eating dessert first so much at dinner those nights ago. It reminded me of him. Of Marcus. He was a good brother."

"And your father?"

"Fair and strong. And very traditional. A man who did not believe in progress for the sake of it. But I admired him greatly. He was very kind. To everyone who worked in the palace. He was fair, even though he could be strict. He was never cruel. He taught me to dance," she said, her voice breaking. "Standing on his feet. I did dance. I lied to you. But it was an easy lie, eh? These truths hurt. These memories."

"He sounds like a good man."

"You would never have had to assassinate him." She laughed. "Though in the end he was, I suppose. His goodness did not save him. It was a terrible lesson. Knowing that being strong and good could not keep you safe. I hated that lesson."

The time it took him to respond spoke volumes of how he listened. It was such a wonderful, strange thing. To share with another person like this.

Yes, she had made friends with her staff at the palace, but they worked for her. It was not the same as this.

"The world is a broken place," he said. "Good people die."

The words were heavy and fragile all at once. And she knew she had been trusted with a truth that resided deep within his soul.

"I know well. My mother, she was… She was beautiful. Tall and elegant. And her hair always looked perfect. She smelled like lilacs and sunshine. A particular perfume, but I do not know it. All memory of my family was eradicated from here. None of their things were kept if they did not have value. Value to *them*. But what had value to them is different than what would've had value to me and…"

"Of course."

"All I have are memories. I remember one time we all went on a picnic. We sat by the lake, and we were happy. We were so happy. Happy to eat together and be together. I will not forget that. It was a gift. It was not long before the coup. I think that is what strikes me now as so desperately unfair. My father was a King. My brother was the heir. My mother was a Queen. But they were just my family. And if we had just been a family they would never have been killed."

"All too often innocents are caught in the cross fire." He shifted, holding her more tightly. "It is a fact of this world that I despise, and one I have fought for years. It does not do good to dwell on the things that you cannot change. Or to ask *what if*. For I have done that. I have done it exhaustively. I have asked why many times and was never met with an answer. Sometimes things simply are."

"Yes. But it is hard not to wonder. How things could be different."

"But that is the path to insanity. Or at least revenge."

"Is that the path you've been on?"

"Yes," he said.

"What happened? I spoke of my family to you... I gave myself to you. Tell me. What is it?"

"My story is not of help to anyone."

"Well," she said, "I don't know that my story is particularly helpful to anyone either. But someone should remember my family. And only I remember them in this way. It is an honor to their memory to speak of them, isn't it?" She waited. Only for a beat. "Maybe you should speak of the woman you lost."

There was a breath. Then her name.

"Stella."

"Stella," she said, testing the name.

She felt a surge of jealousy, and she felt also that it was unfair. She didn't know why she should have it either. He was in her bed, and that was enough. She didn't need anything more.

She only needed to listen. As he had done for her.

As they built a web of intimacy together.

"I fell in love with Stella when I was very young. I had no aversion to marrying. My parents had a wonderful marriage. *Have* a wonderful marriage. Long and healthy. Functional. I always thought… I would find the right woman, and I would marry her. Quickly and easily. For love always seemed quick and easy to me. Why wouldn't it? After all, my parents lived a fantasy. Why wouldn't I live the very same fantasy? Love came quickly. It came easily. And it was lost just as quickly and easily. And my life… My life was never what I thought it would be."

"Sorry," she said, her heart squeezing tight. It was not language barriers that made words ineffectual, not now. It was the fact there were no words for these things. For the deep sadness and unfairness in the world. She hated this. Hated that he had been through so much pain. Why did it feel like this?

She didn't think she could recall ever feeling quite so sorry for another person's tragedy. And at the same time she felt…angry. Angry because part of her wished that she could have been loved half so dearly as this

Stella woman had been. But Stella was gone, and Annick lived.

What a very strange thing. Everyone who had ever loved Annick was gone. And this man loved a woman who was not here. It left behind a broken Annick. A broken Maximus. How much more right the world would have been if Annick were gone and Stella were here.

But Annick wanted to be here. Wanted to be in Maximus's arms, in his bed. Annick wanted to be the one who was here, breathing next to him, touching him.

Yes, that was what she wanted. Even if it meant the world remained broken and out of sorts.

She was sorry, though. That a man so beautiful should be so haunted.

She wondered if anyone felt so sorry for her. If anyone looked at her and thought it sad that someone so young had been robbed of so much life.

She didn't know that they did. But either way, she cared for him. Cared for his brokenness. Even if no one much minded her own.

Even if he didn't.

"What happened?"

"My father is not quite the self-made businessman he appears to be. Oh, he is responsible for the way that his life has gone, but he's done things..."

"What things?"

"He engaged in a host of shady business practices initially. My father is a good man in many ways. You have to understand that. As a boy, Dante was living on the streets, tried to rob my father and kill him. And rather than extracting punishment from him, my father sent Dante to a school where he was educated. Took care of him. Introduced him to me. Gave me a lifelong friend who is truly more like a brother. My father also promised my sister to a King in return for aid to his business. And he made bad bargains with the wrong people. And those people sought their revenge when my father thought he could outrun them. When he thought he could cheat them. My father is a family man. He has never been unfaithful to my mother. He raised us well. But he waded into dark waters to create his fortune. And those things have a way of coming back to haunt you. And they did. They did. There was a man sent to punish my father. Sent to kill his son."

"Maximus…"

"But the assassin's bullet did not hit his son." The word broke, along with his voice.

"It hit Stella. I didn't protect her. I couldn't protect her. I didn't know. I was naive. Ignorant. Innocent in a way. I believed that my father was a good man. I believed that he would never do anything to put his children in harm's way. But he did. And worst of all, we didn't know it. Because I didn't know it, I didn't know that Stella was ever in danger by being with me. Her murder remains listed as unsolved. Because the man was an international hit man. And she was just… She was just a girl. A young, beautiful girl who had the misfortune to fall in love with the wrong man, who was connected to the wrong people. She deserved more. She deserved better. She sure as hell deserved to live."

"And all this is for her. All of this," Annick said. "Even protecting me."

"I could see her face when you told me about your plight. She would've been angry with me for abandoning you. She was a good person."

"And you loved her."

"Yes. Of course, then I thought… I thought that love was simple. And that people were exactly who they appeared to be. That love was easy and life was charmed. That my father's legend was real. None of it was real."

"You have a family," she said. "A family who loves you."

He nodded slowly. "That's the truth of it. I do. I have a family—you don't. It must be difficult to have lost your family. Though in some ways I felt that day that I lost mine. At least, my illusion of what it was."

"Me," she said, "I would rather have an illusion than nothing. Than a life spent in the dungeon. I'm not saying it is easy, this. This thing that happened to you. This thing that you learned about your father. But I know what it is to be left with no one. No one to care about your pain. Did your father at least care?"

"He was broken by it. I've never seen a man weep like he did, not even me. Not even me when she died. But he made me swear that I wouldn't tell. Not my mother. Not Min or Violet. And not Dante."

"So they could keep the family they always thought they had."

"My kindness was not for him. But for them."

"It makes sense, this. But then, you're all alone. Maximus King to them. They don't know you. They don't know who you are."

"No. They don't."

"You are in a dungeon. One that you have fashioned for yourself from the stone blocks of your secrets. Maximus King, you fill me with great sadness."

"Don't be so dramatic. I'm not in any kind of prison. I'm here of my own free will. No one has forced me into anything."

"I did. With chloroform."

"You are far too proud of your chloroform, Annick. I could have left at any time if I wanted to."

"Can you? Would you always see bars?"

"See bars?"

"It is reading I did," she said. "About kittens."

"And what do kittens have to do with bars?"

"It is what kittens have to do with us, I think. If they are raised in cages, even when they are freed they see the bars before their eyes. They do not truly ever see themselves as free. They know captivity. They exist in it even after the walls are removed. Do we do that? I wonder."

"People? Or us specifically?"

"You and me." She put her hand first on her chest, then on his. "Maximus and Annick."

"I'm just doing what I can to make the imbalance of the world right again. It takes a lot of bad being removed to begin to make up for Stella being gone."

Annick nodded gravely. "She must've been very good, your Stella. To lay claim to your heart once and forever."

"She was."

"She is not using your heart, though. And you could maybe use the return of it."

"It isn't that simple."

She shrugged. "Me, I find most things are actually quite simple."

"Yes, but that simplicity is unique to you, Annick. You act as if you can just say whatever you want. Do whatever you want. Chloroform whoever you want, and it will fix your problems."

"Ah, my life is not so complicated. I might have felt like I could not be myself, but at least I knew what to do. Survive. That is a very simple life. To survive. It is this wanting that I find complicated, Maximus King."

"What is it you want?"

There were many things she wanted, but few of them were possible. For now, she would stick with possible. "I think...more pastries. And then I will have some more of your body."

"Is that so?"

"It is so," she said, nodding definitively.

She couldn't fix the past, not for either of them. But for the moment she felt soothed. For the moment she felt like she might even have a real friend. She was sad for him. For all that he had lost. But it made him kindred in a way. In a way that no one else she knew was or could be. He was broken. Missing pieces of himself. And so was she.

"Then that is what you shall have."

CHAPTER ELEVEN

THEY WERE TO be married the next day. Neither of them had seen the point in tarrying over the planning of the wedding. It was for security. And it needed to be done. Whatever else she might think about necessity, he knew that she understood that. His family had also arrived. They would be staying for a time after the ceremony, and there really was nothing he could do to persuade them otherwise. Annick, for her part, was pleased. And if he were a different man, he might find it charming.

"It is just that there has not been family in this palace for a very long time," she explained, when expressing her delight about his family coming to visit. And he found he could not begrudge it to her.

She was so fragile. And yet so determinedly strong all at once. Annick and her chloroform. He had never intended to get himself embroiled in this sort of thing. Had never thought that he would get married. Most especially not after Stella. His love for her had been branded on his soul. Initially. Now what he did was not out of blind grief. It had left him in doubt of eternal love.

Because he didn't feel that love anymore. He didn't feel her close to him. That year he had spent loving her could do nothing to close the gap of the sixteen years spent without her. And so, revenge, balancing the scales, that was his quest. It was nothing to do with love. And the things he had learned about his father in the aftermath of it all…

It had twisted everything he thought about the world. Losing Stella had been more than simply losing her. It had meant a change to the way that he saw absolutely everything.

Annick made him feel something.

He did not care for it.

He had shared with her, though, and that had… It had moved things onto strange and shaking ground. There was a connection that he felt with her unlike anything he had experienced before, and that had not been the way this was meant to be.

He was supposed to protect her.

He was supposed to be helping her.

He was not supposed to be affected by her.

"Well, this really is quite something."

He turned where he stood in the entry to the castle, just in time for his sister Violet and her husband, Javier, to walk through the door. Violet was pregnant and looking glowing. It did something strange to him, to see his younger sister grown in this way. He'd been through it already with Minerva, though it had come out later that the child she had come home from a semester abroad with was not actually her child, but the child of a friend who had needed rescuing. As if thinking of her conjured her up, Minerva came in as well, also pregnant. Dante was with her, carrying their adopted daughter in his arms. And behind them came Robert and Elizabeth King, his parents, who looked tan, fit and remarkably well-preserved. As always.

"This is incredible," Minerva said. "You both live in such splendid palaces."

"*Cara,*" Dante said. "Are you disappointed that I have not bought you a palace? Because

I could. Would you prefer an atmospheric ruin in the Highlands? One with a very large library..."

"Yes," she said. "Would you really buy me a castle?"

"And a pony if you so wish."

His eyes glittered with humor. And Maximus was surprised to discover how pleased he was with that. His friend had been beset by darkness for years. And Minerva seemed to have brought him out of it. He never would've thought that. He would have said that Min was too shy. Too bookish. But she had done wonders for him. He didn't know the Prince that Violet had married, but he had it on good authority that sunny, flashy Violet had done much the same for him.

He thought of his own fiancée. Wide-eyed, determined, and no less tortured than he was.

His sisters had brought with them a sense that the world could be right. And they had given it to those men that cared for them so.

He could bring nothing of the kind to Annick. And she would hold no magic elixir of healing for him.

They had seen too many dark things. They

knew too many hideous truths about the world.

"Well, it's good to see all of you," Maximus said, working to put his mask in place. He wouldn't have to explain that to Annick, which was a blessing. Because Annick understood. Annick knew.

He felt a ripple go through his family, and he turned. Annick was standing in the doorway, wearing her crown and a silver gown that wrapped around her curves.

Annick had taken this dressing-for-how-she-wanted-to-appear thing to heart. Intensely. She was nothing if not blatantly over-the-top at every opportunity.

"Hello," she said.

"Your Majesty." His mother curtsied.

"Your Highness," came from his father.

Minerva curtsied and Dante inclined his head. Javier and Violet stepped forward, shaking Annick's hand. "Your Highnesses," Annick said. "It is good of you to come and grace my country."

"A pleasure," Javier said. "For I know full well how good it is to be able to share your country with the world after many years of it being on the brink of devastation. My own brother has just reformed our native land of Monte Blanco to a glorious state. And you are more than welcome to come for a visit."

"I should like that," Annick said. "I should love to speak to you about all the things that you have done to fix the...atrocities that were visited upon your people. I am working diligently to try and make right what has happened to mine. But it is not so simple always."

"It never is."

"Indeed not," Violet chimed in. "Sometimes they must kidnap someone to accomplish their ends."

"It makes for an interesting story at parties," Annick said. "A slightly more interesting story about how we met than many others have, don't you think?"

Violet laughed, and the rest of his family too. Clearly utterly charmed by this rather serene version of Annick that stood before them.

It was not a part she was playing. And yet she was also not the urchin he'd held in his arms the night before, who had told him dirty jokes, then happily ate pastries in bed and wiped her buttery fingers against his bare chest.

It was all of her, fused into one formidable being.

And it was a sight to behold.

"That is true." Violet shrugged. "And I have the added bonus of being able to tell people that I was kidnapped specifically so that I could marry his brother. And ended up marrying him myself."

"We're interesting if nothing else," Javier said.

"Quite," Annick agreed.

"We shall have dinner," Maximus said. "First, you may all find your bedrooms and put your things away."

"Will you come with me?" Violet said, smiling. "It's just that I have packed so many things, and I would hate to inconvenience your staff."

"What about your husband?"

"Oh, I'll inconvenience him plenty. It's only that I still need more arms than that."

Leave it to Violet to have packed an entire castle.

He followed his sister back out to the front of the palace, and she rounded on him.

"Are you in trouble? Blink twice if you need to leave."

"It was my idea," he said.

"Marriage was your idea?"

"Yes," he said. "It was. She needs help. I'm not marrying her under sufferance."

"Well, you can leave. We'll get you diplomatic immunity. Whatever you need."

"Whatever you need," Javier agreed.

"I don't *need* anything. I promise. Anyway, it's entirely possible Annick is pregnant with my child. So I should probably stick around." He knew the act he put on contributed to his family's response to this. Had they truly known him, they wouldn't have been half so worried.

"Oh, good God," Violet said. "You are such a man whore that you had to have sex with the woman who kidnapped you?"

He looked pointedly at his sister's baby bump. "What kind of person would do such a thing?"

"It's different," Violet said. "Isn't it?"

"I don't know."

"Do you love her?"

He looked at his sister. "No."

"Then why are you doing this?"

"I don't need to be in love, Violet. I don't want to be."

"Is this because of Stella?"

He knew his sister couldn't remember Stella well. She'd been too young. But Violet knew that their father wasn't perfect. He'd sold her in marriage, after all. But she didn't know about this. And he wasn't going to explain.

"That was sixteen years ago. And things have changed. I am who I am."

"So you're going to marry that beautiful creature and never love her?"

That stung. But this wasn't the moment to worry about Annick's emotions. He was here to protect her. He was marrying her to protect her. That was it.

"Annick has a life to get to living. I'm not going to hold her back. Not when it's her chance to be free."

"And your chance to maintain the status quo. Congratulations."

He rounded on his sister. "And what do you mean by that exactly?"

"I think you know. You found yourself a stunning woman who isn't going to demand fidelity of you. And you get to be a King. Must be fun. And the bonus is that you get to rehab the image of the country. But what about you? Do you ever get deeper than image?"

"And where exactly is all this coming from?" he asked.

"It just seems to me that you found yourself a sort of ideal situation."

"And yet you don't sound happy for me."

"Well, no. Because actually… I hoped for better for you."

"You don't know me, Violet. Not as well as you think."

"Whose fault is that?"

"It wasn't an accusation," he said. "Merely an observation."

His sister produced a purple velvet trunk, which he picked up off the ground and slung over his shoulder, walking back toward the palace. He didn't need lectures from Violet on how he might proceed with his life. She didn't know the half of it. Didn't know the half of him. He strolled back into the palace and saw Annick standing there. Their eyes met. Annick was the only person who did know. His whole family, the people he had grown up with. His parents who had raised him… They didn't know. Only this woman knew. This woman he had known for a couple of weeks. He didn't quite know what to do with that realization. So he simply walked on. Tonight, they would have dinner. Tomorrow, they would be married. And it didn't matter what Violet had to say about it. It was set in stone. It would not change.

CHAPTER TWELVE

ANNICK FELT STRANGE, sitting there with his family. Knowing what she did about his father, and that no one else knew it. And just… being around the family. It was a strange and layered thing. Shot through with moments of exhilaration and happiness and deep, unsettling grief. She felt quite unlike herself.

Unable to find a retreat inside of herself to go to as she normally did. Unable to protect herself against the sheer domesticity of what was happening in the palace.

A palace that had not seen such a thing since the death of her family.

"Violet and Maximus have always been the excessive ones," Min was saying. "And I was the one that everyone overlooked."

"Not everyone, *cara*."

Minerva laughed at her husband. "Oh, you most of all. Don't try to rewrite history now, Dante. Anyway, if you would have noticed me a moment before it was appropriate, my father would've had you killed."

"Unless I did it first," Maximus said, smiling that charming grin that she knew was fake. What was real was the threat underlying his words. She knew that he wasn't lying. Or exaggerating. Except that… He would've done it himself. If a man had done anything to harm one of his sisters, she had full confidence that Maximus would be the one to handle the insults all on his own.

"It's good you have Maximus here with you, Annick," Robert King said. "He's always been brilliant. Since you're trying to accomplish reform here in the country, I know he'll do right by you and your people."

Annick studied him closely. He did seem a very nice man, as Maximus had said he was. He was of indeterminate age, obviously old enough to have Maximus as a son, but still difficult to pinpoint. His wife even more so, her face dramatically lacking in lines. They were a beautiful family. Violet stunning, Minerva an understated mourning dove. Elizabeth King the sort of blonde beauty that all celebrities aspired to.

She could see how Maximus had felt like he lived a charmed life. And how badly it would've hurt to have had that challenged. To have lost that in any regard.

"Yes," Annick said, looking directly at the older man. "He's quite brilliant. And I think…much more than anyone realizes." She could feel his warning glare burning into the side of her face. "I'm quite lucky to have him."

"Anyone would be," Robert King agreed.

Dinner was served then, a basket of pastries coming out before the meal. Annick smiled.

"Is this a tradition here?" Minerva asked.

"No," Annick said happily. "Well, I suppose it will be."

By the end of it all, the tension she felt toward even his father was forgotten, because she felt surrounded by this love that she had not been near for years.

And she wanted so desperately to be part of it. She wanted so desperately to belong to someone. Wanted so much to be…

She cut that thought off. It did no good to dwell on the things she did not have control over. It did no good to wish for the clock to reverse. To wish for life to be different. She had done it hundreds of times. She knew it did no good.

She had lived the life she did. That was all.

Tomorrow she would marry into this family. Something that she could never have foreseen. Something entirely different to the life she had imagined loomed ahead of her. Tomorrow, things would change.

When dinner was done, she excused herself, and she didn't even wait for Maximus. She found herself wandering away from the bedrooms. Away from the ballroom. Away from every civilized part of the castle, to a place that she hadn't been back to since the day that she had been set free.

Her heart constricted in her chest as she made her way down the dark, narrow steps. As she descended down a level, and then another. All the way to the lower dungeon.

This place was a reminder. Of where she had come from. Of what really mattered. It wasn't her feelings or his family or...

Her dungeon lay untouched since she'd been freed.

It needed to stand. As it was. At least, it felt to her it did.

It was not a grimy jail cell. It was a room. With a bed in the corner. No windows. It was dingy, not clean. Atop her small nightstand a copy of the Bible and *Anne of Green Gables* sat there still, the two books that she had read the most during her isolation, as they were the only ones perennially left behind by her tutor. There was a small desk in the corner, which had also been there since the beginning. And nothing more. She felt small here. That trembling sensation that she'd always battled in her chest loomed large.

"What are you doing down here?"

"I… I might ask you the same thing?"

"I followed you."

"I did not give you permission to do so."

"Since when have I needed your permission for anything?"

"This is not to share." Tears filled her eyes. "I want you to go away."

"Is this where they kept you?"

"It is not your…"

"Is this where they kept you, Annick? In

this room like a...like a patient at a mental ward?"

"Yes," she said.

"This is...disgusting."

"It is," she agreed.

"I would go back and kill them all over again if I had not already done so," he said, his tone black as night. "How dare they do this to you."

"It is so. They did it. I suppose it does not matter how."

"It matters to me."

"I felt so different sitting around your family, I thought perhaps I would come down here and see if I was. But I'm the same. I tremble standing here. Afraid that I will not be able to choose to leave." She turned around. "But the bars are not there. You are." He filled the doorway, his large frame taking up all that space once occupied by the locking door.

"How did you survive it?"

"The way we all survive such things. We go to whatever place inside of ourselves we can find that will protect us. Keep us safe. You have this place. This place you go to when you smile with charm to your parents. Or maybe it is the place you go when you pick up your gun to kill the men who you imagine are the ones who killed Stella. It is what you do, yes? Every time. That man becomes the man who killed her."

"This is not about me."

"It is about those of us who live on. When we sometimes wish we had not. That is what this is. We are not so different, Maximus King."

"This prison cell is a damn horror," he said, looking around.

"My life was a 'damn horror,' as you say. And yet somehow I am here. As are you."

"Let's go upstairs."

"We are to be married tomorrow. And I am Queen." Unexpectedly, a tear slid down her cheek. "I did not ever think I would live to see this day. A wedding day. The day that I wore the crown. It is all hitting me now. After all these years of hiding. All these years of feeling nothing. It is all hitting me now. All these feelings that were locked away here. How can you even have feelings in here?"

"You can't," he said. "This place is torture all on its own."

"Yes. It is so. But it is a torture I survived. To come out of this place. To this moment." She looked at him and her heart ached. It felt too heavy. Much too heavy. And suddenly, she wanted to run from him as badly as she wanted to run from the cell. Because... What she really wanted, standing there, raw from that dinner she had just shared with his family, she could admit wounded her just as much.

She wished that she could be loved. It was a terrible thing that Maximus grieved Stella so much. But... But what a wonderful thing to be grieved. What a wonderful thing to have someone love you quite so much that they turned their life inside out, that they became a mythical beast on your behalf, attempting to rid the world of injustice just so you might be avenged.

She had no idea what that sort of love must be like.

Years. She had spent years in this room. With captors who were utterly and completely dispassionate about her. Captors who didn't care if she lived or died. Who trotted her out when it was necessary. Who used her to support their great and terrible acts. Who only educated her, even just the slightest, so that she could put on a performance of being cared for.

She was so hungry for love. There were so many things to grieve about the loss of her family, but the deepest one, the deepest one that she had not wanted to acknowledge for all this time, was that when she lost them she had also lost the only people who cared about her.

The only people in the world who loved her.

And she had him, this dark avenging angel, but he was not *her* dark avenging angel.

He was avenging the wrongs committed against another. And he was using her as a token for that, but it still wasn't the same.

It still wasn't…love.

"I am tired," she said. "And I must ready myself for our wedding. I should not like to be a hideous bride."

"You could never be hideous," he said.

"I am, I think, cursed with faint praise, eh?"

"You will be nothing but beautiful," he said, his voice too smooth, his smile too easy. He was playing a part again.

Why? Because all of this was too real for him?

He ran, when things were intense. When they shared. Even if his body was here, his soul was running and she knew it.

"Says Maximus King? Or the King?"

"I don't know what you're talking about."

"Ah, the Playboy. How nice for me. I will meet him again at the altar tomorrow. And he had better look exceptionally sharp. Had better do me proud. In my country."

"As trophy husbands go, you have a very good one."

"And one who could ward off the threat without so much as breaking a sweat. I am quite fortunate, I think."

"You look angry."

"I am angry. All the time. Aren't you?"

And tired. Just so damn tired.

"I'll see you in the morning. My very angry bride."

"See you then."

But when she went to sleep, she no longer felt filled with that momentary joy she'd experienced. That sense of wonder that she was getting more than she had ever imagined she might. Now she felt overwhelmed by the realization that what she wanted was the love of the man who had no heart left to give. The love of a man who did not even know who he was.

And wanting Maximus's love was as impossible as wanting the love of her parents.

For when he said that his love, his heart, was gone, she believed it.

So she wrapped herself up in a blanket on her bed and then wrapped herself even deeper in a blanket of impossibility and futility, and she would not allow herself to weep.

CHAPTER THIRTEEN

IT WAS A beautiful day for a wedding. Too bad she still felt so terribly sad. But her gown was sensational, and even though her heart was sore, she looked like she ought to.

It was only her feelings that were not quite where she hoped they would be.

She had thought a lot about those feelings. Love. Of course, it was natural that she wanted love. But that did not mean she was *in* love with him.

That would be the saddest thing of all. It was only that she was lonely. And when he held her, it felt like something special. It was good she had not let him hold her last night. His arms contained a kind of magic that made her feel happy, but also sadder all at once.

And now they would be married.

She walked down to the chapel all on her own. It was different than the day of the coronation, when she had had Maximus to escort her. She held the bouquet of flowers that had been provided for her and looked down at the blossoms. A curl of blond hair fell into her face as she did, and she felt a strange cracking sensation about her heart. Her father should have been here. He should have been here to give her away. To place her on the arm of Maximus King, a man who would care for her. She felt a presence behind her. And she turned. It was Maximus.

"Are you ready?"

"Aren't you meant to be inside?"

"Probably. But I came to find you."

Her heart nearly flew from her chest. He came to find her.

She remembered being in that dungeon room. Being in the dark. Seeing him.

Knowing somehow that he would be her salvation, but she had not known it would be this.

Even though she had been too afraid to do it at the time, she reached her hand out for him, and he took it.

He was here.

He had come to find her, just now.

He would be her husband and she... She was happy about that.

"I was only thinking of my father," she said softly. "It is not so much that I need a man to give me away. I do not. It is that a father cares for his children. For his daughter. And when he gives her to a man, he is giving her to a man he believes will care for her, if all is well. My father died in fear of the safety of his children. I am safe. I wish he could see. I wish that he could have given me to you, rather than seeing me stolen away by the men who then killed him. Though perhaps in his last moments it was not his concern."

"The ones you love are always your concern," Maximus said.

There was a flower pinned to the lapel of his suit jacket, and he snapped it off then. Then he placed it down on the stone wall right beside the entry to the church. "For your father."

Tears filled her eyes and she broke a blossom off the top of her bouquet, then another. And she set them beside the first. "My mother and Marcus."

"Do you know," he said. "I never was a big believer in the afterlife. And spirits. And living on. But I know that it is Stella who guides me sometimes. My memory of her, her spirit, whichever you like to call it. They see you."

She closed her eyes and nodded slowly. "Thank you."

Maximus looked to the flowers. "I will keep her safe. I swear it with my life. If you were here, you would approve this match. You would know that I was sincere. That when I make vows I keep them. And I make this a vow. Annick will come to no harm as long as I am here. I would give my life for hers."

Annick shivered. But she couldn't speak.

"Shall we go in?" he asked.

"Yes," she said.

He took her arm, and he led her up the aisle, as he had done for the coronation. The priest was there waiting, just as he had been then too, but Maximus stood with her. And these vows were not to the country, but to each other. The traditional vows always spoken at weddings in Aillette.

"The world is full of hard places," she said

slowly, reading from the paper she held in her hands. "But I will be soft for you. The world is full of uncertainty, but I will be constant. The world is out there, and we are here. And in my heart, you have become the world."

When Maximus spoke, his rich voice filled the room, vibrated with her soul.

"The world is filled with danger, and I will be your strength. Your weapon. Your sword and your shield. I will be your guard. I will be your warrior. I will protect you and preserve you, for my life is yours. And my world is here."

She was not supposed to believe it. It was not supposed to matter. Not quite to the degree that it did. But oh, how she wished she could. How she wished she could freeze all of this and hold it to her chest.

And when they were introduced as the sovereign rulers of Aillette, King Maximus and Queen Annick, she felt the strangest sense of wholeness. Of unity. She looked at him, and she looked out in the crowd, at the King family watching them, clapping for them.

Applauding as if this was a common American affair.

And she felt…part of something. Part of a family. And Maximus had even included her parents. Had spoken vows to their spirits. And suddenly she didn't feel so alone. And it was that hope inside of her that frightened her the most. That need.

Oh, how could she have ever talked herself into believing she did not love him? This beautiful, broken man who she had spirited away with the aid of chloroform, but who had turned the power around when he demanded marriage. This man who was trying to right wrongs that simply could not be fixed. This man made from lies and vengeance and a deep, unending love for another woman.

She loved him.

She did. There was nothing to be done for it. Nothing that could make it go away. And she didn't even want it to. Because last night she had revisited that dungeon, and it was isolation. The bars were gone, and Maximus was there instead. Though he might be his own kind of prison. Yes, loving him might be its own kind of hell.

They were swept off to the reception. A large white tent lay out on the lawn. And she had never felt quite so broken or quite so happy in all of her life.

Her people were here, eating and smiling and free. It all made sense then. How she could live for them and herself. How those two things were not at odds. How she could love Maximus with deep ferocity and love them as well. How she could love him and expect nothing in return, but also want it desperately. How she could wish to devote herself to this country, but also wish to be a wife, and a mother to whatever children they had. Children who would also be both property of the country, and property of themselves. It was a difficult life, this. And one thing she was certain of when she stood there watching it all was that it took more courage and more love, and not less. You could not lead if you did not contain all these things. Not well. Not right.

And so it might be dangerous. To care like

this. But if she did not, if she held back, if she tried to protect herself, then it would be like living in a dungeon. For then, in that life, she had held back everything that she believed, everything that she felt, simply because she had to protect herself. That had been a matter of life and death, but this was not. She could not hold back these feelings. To do so would make her a lesser Queen. To do so would make her less than Maximus deserved.

He had believed in love at one time. And all that he thought about the world had been destroyed. Cruelly. Could she not give him a piece of it back? She wanted to. Oh, how she desperately wanted to. For her Maximus King. Her King. Her husband.

Her love.

And she somehow knew innately that after today he would try to resist her. Because of course he would. It was the way of him. He drew close, and then away. What was he afraid of?

Feeling. She knew.

He was adamant that he had no heart left,

but everything she had seen of him suggested otherwise.

The way that he stayed with his family, even with the issues he had with his father... No, he was not a man with no heart. Not a man with no soul.

He was a man with so much love to give, so bright and brilliant, like the sun that had been hidden from her for all those years. And it was nearly too much for her to bear. But also, she was sensitive to it. More perhaps than most because she had been kept in the darkness for so long. Because she had been kept away from people. And this thing between them... It was magic. It was more than necessity.

More than sex. She was certain of it.

She tried to remember back to when she had thought that sex was merely an appetite, as he had said. That he was a pastry she could go about sampling before she had another, and she realized what a foolish thing that was. There would never be another. Not for her. It was this broken man. With her. All broken. Together.

Yes, life was filled with tragedies, but looking at him now, she felt all of the miracles it contained as well. For he was a miracle to her.

She only hoped that she could be one for him.

And she would not let him pull away. Not tonight. Not on the night of their wedding.

She might have been a virgin only recently, but she was not afraid to seduce him.

She was not afraid to show him what was in her heart.

He had taught her about food, and the pleasure she might find there. His body, and all the joys that it contained. And now perhaps she would teach him about love. In the way that she understood it.

Love after brokenness.

After all these gifts he had given to her… Could she do anything less for him?

The wedding had left him feeling grim. Yes, it had been his idea, and yes, he had made many a bold declaration inside of himself that a wedding meant nothing, but he found it seemed less true than he would like.

By the end of the evening Annick was

tired, he could tell. So when all the guests had left, he took himself off to his own chamber. He had a need for distance. His family was still in residence, and interacting with them was always a chore. Being that charming playboy that he was so accustomed to being... It was becoming a chore.

So what are you, then? The soldier?

He feared that it might be true.

That everything about Maximus King was simply a shell. That the one who was real was a man who took orders, carried out missions other men shied away from.

The one who pulled the trigger without mercy when necessary. The one who existed in a space between revenge and vigilante justice.

He had done good, but the question was, how much did he even care about it anymore?

If he were honest, he had lost that connection to Stella at some point over the years.

He no longer felt that deep, aching grief that he once had for her. No longer felt as if she was some sort of eternal love, a guiding light.

No. All had become darkness at a certain stage. Except Annick.

When he had walked Annick down the aisle today, when he had seen her in her gown, she had been light.

And he felt...reluctant to touch her. Like if he put his hands on her snow-white dress he would leave behind oily dark fingerprints. Or perhaps blood.

There was blood on his hands and he couldn't even bring himself to feel guilty about it. And that bothered him more than anything.

At first... At first it had had a cost. Killing. At first, he had felt the weight of every life he had taken. Yes, it was no different than war. These military operations. He knew that; he understood it. Many men did such things. They fought for the safety of their country, the lives of their countrymen, and what he was doing was that. He killed dictators' investments. Assassins. Murderers. None of them were innocent. But at a certain point, he had lost his own claim to innocence. He might be able to justify each and every thing he had done, might be able to weigh it against the lives those men would have eventually taken. But it did not make him a saint. It did not make him right.

He wondered sometimes if he was simply a man in darkness, the same as all of them. Choosing a side, and deciding it was right.

If the right evidence had been presented to him, would he have been involved in the removal of Annick's father?

He wanted to say no. But there had come a point where he had chosen who he believed. About who was good and who was evil.

No, he never, ever would have harmed a woman or child, but even so.

He had questions about his own frailty.

And he wished to drown those questions away in alcohol tonight. Not in Annick.

There was a knock at his chamber door, and she appeared. As if he had conjured her up with the pour of the whiskey. Whiskey like he had on the plane.

Whiskey, which Annick claimed she never had.

Oh, Annick, far too innocent for him. Far too much of a soft, undeniable beauty. That was, he supposed, the trade-off of her being locked away in that abysmal room. She had not been able to touch the outside world, and it had not been able to touch her.

"What are you doing here?"

"What is this? This stupid question. Why do you think I'm here?"

"For a drink?"

"No. An insult, Maximus, that you think I'm here for anything other than my wedding night."

"Such a traditionalist," he said, fighting against the rising tide of lust that was taking hold. Doing away with any kind of defenses he'd put up.

He had promised her family he would care for her, and this vow he'd made to the dead felt binding. But it was heavy. For how could he be sure he would not fail her? How?

"Don't take it as an insult."

"I have."

"I'm not in the mood."

She looked at him, all narrowed eyes and indignation. "Me, I think you're a liar."

"Of course I'm a liar. A liar," he said, advancing on her. "A liar who shows a mask to the whole world." He took another step closer to her, a dangerous heat rising up inside of him. "A drunk." He lifted his glass. Then he took another step toward his bride, so close that he could smell the lovely, enticingly feminine scent that he associated only and ever with her. "A killer."

"Yes," she said softly. "All these things. And me? I am broken. Grieving. Tragic. Ruthless. Innocent. Guilty. We are all a great many things, are we not?"

"Don't test me tonight," he said.

"It is for just that reason that I test you. Because you don't wish it. Who wants to test a man who is prepared for that test? Boring."

"Are you in danger of being bored?"

"Not with you. Never with you." She closed the door behind her. "Also, I am not leaving. You do not scare me, Maximus King. I suppose I am now Annick King. You have made me a King as well." Her lips tugged into a smile. "And a Queen. A strange thing."

"I did not think a Queen would take the name of the man she married."

"Maybe not in public. But in private, I would like to do so. I have no family. I like very much the idea of being part of yours."

That brushed against that raw, deadly thing inside of him. "Whatever you wish."

"And if I wish for my wedding night?"

"Unwise," he said, tipping back the last of his whiskey.

"You keep saying this. As if there is a monster in you, waiting to savage me at the first available moment. But I have not met this monster. What would you say if I told you that I would like to meet him?"

"You don't."

"Why not? Did your Stella meet the monster?"

"Stella," he said, his voice rough, "didn't meet the monster because I was just a man when I was with her. Just one man. Not... whatever I have become."

"Good," Annick said. "I want to be the first. You were my first. Let me be yours."

"There have been many women."

"But none of them have met the real you, have they? No one has. Not your family... and even with me you hold back."

"I saw the dungeon that you lived in for all of your life. I feel sorry for you. I pity you. I would never put you in an even more pitiable position by exposing you to everything I am."

"And me, I'm not fragile. You know what I've seen. The same things you have. The life of the ones I love drained away right before my eyes. How could you think that I am someone who needs to be protected from monsters? Maybe I am a monster as well. Maybe we all are, given the right circumstances. Maybe that is the real secret. That we are all of us capable of anything if pushed. I kidnapped a man and dragged him across the world in spite of the fact that I spent many years being held prisoner. You would think I would not be able to do so, but I did. When feeling desperate. Because we are all human. We just lie, all the time, about what it means to be human."

"This is your final warning."

He could feel the beast within pulling at the chains. He would give her something to be afraid of if she wasn't careful.

"I do not do what I'm told anymore." And then she unzipped that wedding gown and let it fall to the floor, revealing her bare, pale body, so fragile and lovely. Soft. Calling to everything that was dark and rough and hideous within him.

He wanted to devour her. Consume her. Make her his own. Utterly and completely. His captive.

His Queen. Did she understand that he was no better than those men that had held her for all those years? She didn't seem to care. She was foolish for him, and it made him angry as much as it satisfied him. He had no real consistency when it came to her, and that bothered him most of all. He didn't know what face to wear, what mask. And that resulted in this feeling that he had no mask at all. A fate that terrified him most of all.

"Give me your darkness."

"No."

"It is in our vows. And I will add to them. Give me your darkness and I will be your light."

"You need all the light you have. If you have any yet remaining inside of you…"

"I will give it how I wish. It is not exhaustible." She reached out and touched his face. "And when it is put up against the darkness, the light wins, Maximus. Every time."

"Annick…"

She pressed her body against his, her face determined. "Take me. Make me yours. You. Whoever he is. The King. Maximus. Someone in between. Or someone much further in the dark. I want to be yours. In a way that no one else ever has been. I want to know you. All of you."

"I have blood on my hands," he said.

"If that is so, let me see it. If that is so, let me decide if I'm strong enough."

"I would spare you."

"Life has not spared me. I was never innocent. You know this. I was created as something strong enough to handle you. Do not dishonor that. Do not dishonor my pain by trying to protect that which is not there."

He growled, unable to resist. Unable to stop himself now. It was done. The thing inside of him loosed. And he grabbed her face, gripped her chin and held her steady as he lowered his head for a kiss. As he consumed her. Claimed her as his own. As he made her his.

She gasped, arching against him as they kissed.

"I want you to be my prisoner now," he said. "How do you like that? How would you like it?" He kissed her neck, all the way down her delicate throat, where he bit her. And she gasped. "Mine. What does that make me? A man who would take you prisoner all over again."

"But I would choose it." She put her hands in front of her, holding her wrists together. And he wrenched his tie from his neck and bound her quickly. Efficiently. A kick of desire ran through him as he saw her like that. A willing supplicant bound for his every desire.

"To your knees."

She obeyed, and he felt… Like there was a knife pressed against his flesh. Pushing deep. Pushing him to see how far he could go. How far he could take this. He began to disrobe. Removing his shirt. Removing the rest of his clothes slowly. Determinedly.

And she knelt there, a pair of white lace panties across her hips, and that black tie a dark slash against her pale wrists.

"Take me into your mouth."

She straightened up, obeying, using her mouth to pleasure him.

"Come now. You can still use your hands."

She raised her bound wrists, cupping his length with her hands as she continued to pleasure him with her tongue.

"Yes, this is what I will do with my prisoner. She will see to my pleasure. To my moods. What do you think of that? Will you enjoy that, my Queen? Being available for my every need? My every desire?"

"I'm yours," she said. "Gladly." And she continued on. Giving to him all that he asked, all that he demanded. He put his hand on the back of her head and began to thrust his hips forward in time with her movements. She made a small sound, but continued to pleasure him. And when he felt his own desire rise to the point that he could no longer hold back, he knew that he should leave her be.

He should not finish it this way. But she wanted the beast. She wanted all of him. She would have him.

He growled, releasing then, and when it was over, she looked up at him, a light of satisfaction in her eyes. "What else do you desire of me?"

He picked her up, carried her to the bed then, laid her out before him, spreading her like she was a delicious feast. It would not take him long to be ready again. That release had not been sufficient to drown out the ache in his gut that existed only for Annick.

"A glutton for punishment?"

"I told you I was a glutton," she said. "It is not my fault you do not believe. Not my fault that you insist on treating me as if I am fragile. Perhaps, had I not been kept in a dungeon, there would've been a great many lovers before you."

He growled, pinning her to the bed. "But I would've been your last."

"Would you?"

"Yes," he said, looking at her with all the ferocity that he felt building in his soul. "And you know what? I'm glad there were no others. Because you are mine." He put his hand between her legs. "Mine."

"Then the return is true. Me, I am possessive. And if this possession is good for you, then it is also good for me."

"Very good." He parted her slick lips with his fingers and pushed one deep inside of her. Watching as her face contorted with pleasure. As he teased her. Loving the silken feel of her. Loving that he was the only man ever to touch her like this. That he would be the only one ever.

He let that sense of possession run wild inside of him. Oh, this woman. How she called to him. How she tempted him, teased and tormented him. He wished to bury himself in her and never come back from it. He wanted to send them both into oblivion. Where there was nothing else and no one else. Nothing but them. Ever.

But he wished to extract every last drop of pleasure from her body first. He lowered himself down between her legs, tasting her as he continued to stroke the inside of her body. As he went on a search for that pleasure point he knew was deep inside, all the while moving his tongue over that sensitized bundle of nerves.

She twisted, arched beneath him, and he used his free arm to hold her to the bed. Her hands were still bound, but that didn't stop her from trying to claw at him.

"Behave yourself," he said, biting her inner thigh, earning himself a sharp cry. He pushed her. Further. Higher. Faster. Until she was sobbing his name. Until the beast within began to roar. Wanting to extract all that he could from her. To make her weak with ecstasy. It would never be enough. This. How could it ever be? He felt the deep, cavernous hole inside of him, and he did not know how he was supposed to fill it. Ever. And so he aided her until she was shaking. Quivering violently against his mouth. Until she shattered around his fingers, until he was so hard he hurt with it, but would not allow himself to sink into her honey depths. Not yet.

He lifted himself, pressing his hardness against that unbearable softness, dragging himself back and forth between her folds. She gasped, reaching toward him with her bound hands, and he took hold of her and forced those hands above her head. "Stay still." He rocked his hips back and forth over her, that slick friction torturous. A tease of what he truly wanted. To be deep inside of her, surrounded by her, rather than just moving against her desire.

"You do not get to take control here. This pace is not for you to set."

She shattered again. And again. So many times that he lost count. And he kept going until she was limp in his arms. Then he took her, turning her onto her stomach, propping her hips up, leaving her face buried in the bedspread, her arms thrown out in front of her, still bound. The image that she made there, a woman in the throes of surrender, to him. It was the most erotic thing he'd ever seen. And he could no longer claim to be dead inside, because his heart beat so fast he thought it might drill a hole through the front of his chest.

He felt too much here. And there were no lines between the two men that he saw himself as. Between Maximus and The King. Between the man and the killer. He just was. He just was, and he felt dirty and monstrous and free all at once. Shame, greater than anything he'd ever known, welled up inside of him. And nearly as quickly, a sense of being home assaulted him as he touched her lower back, dragged his palm over her perfect ass and brought his fingers down between her thighs to rub her gently. She whimpered.

"Is it too much for you?"

"Never," she said, her voice muffled but defiant. "I am not weak. Me, I am not easily brought down."

"Good."

He positioned himself at her slick entrance and thrust home. He was blinded by it. And he could no longer play games. He gripped her hips hard as he pounded himself inside of her. Lost himself completely in the sweetness of her body. In the rhythm of her cries of pleasure.

"Maximus," she whispered. "I love you."

He nearly stopped then, but it was too late. Those words grabbed hold of him. His throat, his heart, and dragged his release from his body. He cried out as his release overtook him. As his need became the only thing. He spilled himself deep inside of her, the roaring in his blood like the howling of wolves. And in that moment, there was nothing. Nothing but her.

He was only one man. The one who had

lost himself in her. The man who was surrounded by Annick. The man that Annick said she loved. And for a blistering, blinding moment there was nothing else. Nothing but his release and hers blending together. Into one seamless moment. A perfect feeling.

"Annick," he growled.

And when it was over, he reversed their positions, brought her on top of him and tried to find his breath. Somewhere in all of that, her words had shifted to a white light. And he could not hear them again, could not see them. He could only feel them. He was in a daze. Like nothing he'd ever experienced before.

"I love you," she said again.

And that time, he moved away from her. His heart turned to stone. For it was something he could not bear and he had no choice. He had to harden himself against it.

"No," he said.

"Why not?"

"It can't be like that between us. How can you say that? After what I've done to you." He reached out and grabbed hold of the bonds on her wrists, removing them.

"How can I say that after you have made me come more times than I can even count? What does this mean? This insanity coming from you?"

"There's more to life than orgasm, Annick, and you should realize that I've used you pretty appallingly."

"In all the ways I have asked," she said, sounding almost triumphant. "I am not foolish, Maximus. And I am not weak. I like these games. Because in them I'm a prisoner, but I am strong. Do you not see how that is powerful? And in these games, you are a monster, but you are a man. You bite me. You push me. But it only gives me pleasure, not pain. Do you not see the freedom we find here in this?"

"Sex games are not real."

"*Games?* It is not games. And it is not different from talking. From being. It is the same. We are what we do here in this bed. It is part of us. And it cannot be separate. We were playing stupid games to pretend that it could be. Me, and all of my talk of desires. About how I would be with many men. I could not. For I am playing a game inside where I pretend that any man could arouse such passions. But I know they could not. It is you. It is you, and the strength that you have brought to me. These changes that you have given me. It is who you are."

Her words hit him hard, with the force of a bullet. How could she speak with such certainty about him when he felt no such certainty about himself?

"Who am I? Do you know the answer to that?"

"It is simple. You are charming. And good. And bad. Very bad. A killer, you are right. Though for good reasons. I am not ignoring pieces of you to construct love. I know it is there. Just as I know your heart is there, whatever you might think."

"You really don't know any of that for a fact. You don't actually know what you're talking about."

"Am I stupid?"

"You know I don't think you are."

"Then why act like I'm stupid when it is you who are scared?"

"I'm a killer, Annick, and I don't regret it. That's who I am. I was a different man once. I loved someone once. And I won't do it again."

"Lies. You love. And you believe in good. You want to say that you don't. You want to believe that you don't, because it is scary to you. I scare you. You don't scare me, Maximus King, and you need to. Because *you* need to scare me away. But I won't be. Because I'm not weak. Because I know what it is when men love only power, and that is not you."

"But I love my anger," he said. "And I love that I have had the freedom to let it run free."

"Fine. But you did not do bad things with it. You did good for the world. Yes, these are unsavory things, but there is war in this world, is there not? You cannot make yourself out to be a villain any more than a general might be. You do more than simply follow orders—you are willing to do what must be done. No, I will not let you recast yourself as a villain simply because it keeps you safe. Simply because you fear what it might mean to let yourself feel."

"I told you, I'm a monster."

"Yes, and I believe you. But I love this

monster. All the pain that you have been through. All the things that have broken you. The things that have left you sharp and jagged and difficult. For I am no different. Broken and sad in some ways, but filled with hope. And I want, more than anything, to live." She looked at him, her eyes filled with sadness. "You have spent years killing for a woman. Will you not live for one?"

"I can only live a half life. And you deserve more than that."

"You go back on our bargain? Now that you have had your way? Now you have married me?"

He looked her in the eyes. "I vowed to stay with you. I vowed to protect you, and I won't break those vows."

"No. Just bind us both in a life where you refuse to love me but accept my love for yourself."

"I would never have asked for it," he said, the words scraping his throat raw. "You're the one who seems insistent on giving it."

"More fool me."

"I can't give more than this." How could

he? His heart was a stone, and what was beneath…

He was battered. Wounded beyond repair.

She deserved someone more. She deserved something more, but the world had given her a broken and lacking life, and him, a broken and lacking man to go with it.

"No. You won't," she said. "Because you are afraid. A coward. So brave. So brave when it comes to doing things. So afraid when it comes to the feeling of them. Don't think I cannot see. I told you. I do not need a bitch. I need a guard. I need my cane."

"Careful," he said, grabbing her wrist then. "Careful before you insult me."

"You insult us both."

She got off the bed and began to gather her things. She dressed slowly, the anger and hurt radiating off her in waves. But she would know someday that he was doing her a kindness by not prolonging this. By not lying. For his part, he wouldn't lie.

"It is an offense, this," she said. "That we have both survived so much, and both traveled through so much darkness, for you to run away from the light when it is offered."

"Annick…"

"I thought you could rescue me, Maximus. But you are the one who needs rescuing. And if you will not take my hand, then I cannot help."

And then Annick slipped from the room, closing the door behind her. And he was left alone.

As it should be.

CHAPTER FOURTEEN

RAGE SWIRLED THROUGH Annick as she went down the halls, heading back toward her room. She felt mortally wounded. She had known that it would be a fight. That all of this would be so much work. But she had thought… She had thought that she would be able to reach him. Truly, she had. She felt nothing but deep regret over this.

It wasn't her own pain. Not so much. It was his.

He still saw the bars. And until he decided not to, there was nothing she could do.

She heard a sound. A sound that was almost no sound, and then the brick beside her head split apart. She screamed, dropping low and crawling to her bedchamber, slamming the door behind her. She didn't know where it had come from. And it was likely that whoever…

Suddenly, there was a hole in her bedroom door.

She lay flat, as flat as she could. Someone was actually trying to assassinate her.

It was happening. And Maximus wasn't here. He wasn't... She heard the sound of a struggle on the other side of the door. A roar, thunderous and terrible. Clattering and banging about. And then it was silent.

"Annick," came the sound of a rough voice.

"Maximus," she said.

"Open the door. It's safe."

She scrambled to her feet and went to the door. And there he was. Half-dressed, a wound on his face. "An assassin. From Lackland. So now you have your answer as to who is your enemy. It wasn't just the other regime they wanted removed. They'll be dealt with. Harshly."

"Maximus..."

"You forget that I know secrets about them. I didn't take the job to get rid of the dictator of this country without getting insurance. It will be dealt with. And you will be safe."

"I..."

"I was distracted, Annick. Because of that,

you nearly paid the price. It will not happen again. Never."

"It was not… It was not anyone's fault—it was only that…"

"It was my fault," he said, his voice rough. "My fault. I will remain here. I will be your guard, but that is all it can be. A husband in name, but not…not in truth. All of tonight I should have been watching. I should have been prepared. But I was not. And you…you nearly died for it."

"I wouldn't trade anything about tonight."

"I would trade everything," he said. "It's nice for you that you're willing to sacrifice yourself, but I never will."

"Maximus…this has nothing to do with anything that—"

"It does. It has everything to do with it. This is finished. We will not discuss it any further."

"You don't get to decide. You don't get to decide everything about my life."

His rejection was so final. So complete. He was still standing in the room but she could feel the separation. Could feel how absolute it was.

His face was stone. And in that moment, he was The King, and none of the man remained.

She did not know how to reach him. Didn't know how to touch him.

And he was no longer going to allow it.

"Then you put us both in prison."

"Better in prison alive and free than dead."

He turned away from her and went back into the corridor. He was barking orders. Demanding to know how this had happened. There was practically a full-scale military operation happening in the front of the palace by the time she took her next breath.

And she just sat on the bed. She started to tremble. She should be most upset about the fact that she had nearly been killed, but she was mostly frightened of what the future looked like without Maximus. He had retreated. Gone away behind this war-general facade.

She knew that she would not be able to take him now. Chloroform would not be sufficient to subdue him. To bring him to her.

No.

If she was ever going to have him, he would

have to choose. And she didn't know if he ever would.

Annick had spent all of her life in a state of hope. She'd had to. If not for the hope inside of her, she would have lost herself completely while she had been captive. But now she could not find it.

Because how could you hope for a man who had no hope for himself?

She had been wrong, perhaps. Perhaps his darkness was so black it drowned out her light.

Annick had never felt so hopeless before.

In the moment, Annick felt like she was Queen of nothing except her own broken heart.

And there was simply no triumph to be had in that.

In the weeks since the attempt on Annick's life, Maximus had waged a full-scale tactical war against any forces that might seek to oppose his Queen. He had made sufficient threats toward Lackland, and he knew that they would not be pursuing her ever again. Already, he had banded together with Monte

Blanco to ensure that the Lacklanders would be punished. That steep sanctions would be introduced.

The alliance that he had with his brother-in-law was strong, and he was grateful for it. He had hardened his heart against everything. Everything but seeing to Annick's safety. Shoring up the borders of the country. Nothing else mattered. Nothing.

And he... He had been a fool. A fool to believe that he could let the beast out. That he could somehow let his guard down for even a moment. Yes, he had been a fool.

He was not even bothering to pretend that he was the man he'd been in California, not anymore. He had transformed. And there was something comfortable about the position. About being a war general.

He was grateful his family had not remained in the country to see the shift, for his energy had to be devoted to this, to her, and he did not have time to waste answering their questions.

Someday, he supposed, they would have to talk.

What mattered now was Annick.

And it distracted him from the tearing weight in his chest over the distance between himself and his Queen.

It was essential. There was nothing else to be done.

He had used not only the political connections that he had through his brother-in-law, but also business connections that he had through his other brother-in-law and best friend. If he could truly call anyone a friend.

Dante must have sensed his black mood, and those sentiments, because it wasn't long before he showed up at the palace unannounced.

"And where have you left my sister?" Maximus asked, looking at his friend.

"At her new castle. With her pony. She's very happy."

"You indulge Minerva."

"I live to indulge Minerva. She was not indulged enough in her life, and frankly, neither was I. Between the two of us, we live an extravagantly spoiled life. She has books and libraries and runs her charity. I have access to her body whenever I want…"

"You seem a smart man, Dante, and yet

you have not picked up on the fact that it is not a good time to test me in any regard."

"Oh, no, I did. It is only that I want to know why. Black moods are typically reserved for me."

"No, it's just that I usually hide mine."

"Fair. What is going on? I don't blame you for tearing a swath through the world after that attempt on your wife's life. But what I do want to know is why you're behaving in quite this way."

"It's none of your business."

"Isn't it? I am your oldest friend. Your only friend. Don't think I haven't watched you fake your way through life all these years. I know that you changed when Stella died. And I might not know all the particulars of it, but you lost yourself. You became only that shallow playboy. Though you were never only that. This… This is actually more the real you. You being an asshole, that is."

"A very good friend you are."

"It's true. So tell me. What is it that's going on?"

"She brought me here to protect her. This is not a love match."

"Well, I say bullshit to that. It's obvious that she loves you."

He gritted his teeth. "She does."

"Then what's the problem?"

"I can't love her."

"You can't love her? This is your version of not loving somebody?" Dante chuckled. "I'm surprised literal heads haven't rolled over this. You're on a warpath, my friend. If this isn't love, what is?"

"Justice," he bit out. "Nothing more than justice."

"Is that so?"

"You're reading into things that are not there."

"Why not love her?"

"Because it's too dangerous. I let my guard down with her. She was nearly killed because I...because I spent the night with her hands tied over her head driving her mindless with pleasure, and then she said she loved me and I was consumed in my own feelings, too much so to pay attention to what was happening."

"I'm sorry—are you blaming sex and feelings for the fact that someone tried to assassinate her? Because her feelings are not what caused someone to attempt that."

"You don't understand."

"No, I don't."

"I was complacent the day that Stella died too."

"You could not have protected Stella. You didn't know what was coming."

"I should have," he said. "I should have known. I should've done something to save her."

"But you didn't. You couldn't have. Hindsight is all well and good, Maximus, but it doesn't change the past."

"People lie to you about who they are," he said. "They lie to you and then…and then it only puts those you care about in danger."

"What are you talking about?"

"My father…he's not everything he appears to be."

"Your father rescued me from a life of… I would be dead by now if it weren't for your father."

"I know. But Stella is dead because of him. Because of his choices."

"If you have a problem with your father, you should talk to him."

"There's nothing to say. There is nothing to say except that actions he made in business created enemies who destroyed my life. And I could never... I could never look at him the same way again."

"Is this about your grief over Stella's death? Or is it about anger toward him? Him disappointing you and abusing your love?"

That made him stop. "It's not."

"I don't know that I believe that. You should talk to him," Dante said.

"We're not a family that talks about their feelings."

"Well, maybe it's high time we did. Because I can see now, Maximus, that you have been living in some kind of private hell and I let you. What kind of friendship is that?"

"Your friendship is not the issue here."

"Well, perhaps it should be."

"This is not your concern. I can handle this alone."

"Clearly you can't. And speaking as someone who lived under a shroud of their own darkness for a very long time, I can tell you that you shouldn't have to. Minerva saved me. Loving her saved me. You can laugh all you want about castles and ponies, and you can recoil in horror at the fact that I'm sleeping with your sister, but I love her. I love everything about her. And she forced me to change. She forced me to heal. And it was the cruelest, kindest thing anyone has ever done for me. She did not leave me to die in my brokenness. Your family gave me so much, Maximus, but not even your father's caring, your mother's love or your friendship healed me. It was Minerva, and the way that she demanded I love her back. She was the one that changed everything. That fixed everything. It was her love. So if you found a woman that is demanding you give her your heart, then you damn well do it. And if something stands in your way, that is the thing that you should destroy, not the love that could be between you."

"You don't understand what kind of man I am."

"I don't need to. Does *she* understand what kind of man you are?"

"She says she does."

"So listen. Believe her."

"Why should I?"

"Because the other choice is a life lived alone. And believe me when I tell you it's not even a half life. Because I'm standing on the other side of it, and I'm telling you."

"Her whole family died. And she says she loves me. The world treated her in the worst possible way, and she still loves me. And I... I was betrayed and I just... I spiraled into darkness, and I think I might like it there. I think I might not have the strength to walk back out. Because when you live in the darkness, nobody sees what you do. You don't have to be accountable for anything. For anyone."

"I can see the appeal. But what's the point of it?" He looked around the room. "Why did you come here in the first place?"

"Because she needed help."

"And that mattered."

"I don't know why in hell it did. Only that it did."

"I think you do know. It's because even then she called to your heart. Because even then you cared, whether you wanted to or not." Dante stared at him. "Talk to your father."

And then his friend was gone, as if he had not flown across the world to see him. A part of Maximus wondered if he had hallucinated the entire thing.

He poured himself a glass of whiskey, and he started to take a drink. But then stopped. He stared down at the amber liquid. And then he reached for his phone and called his father.

"Hello?"

"I blame you for Stella's death."

There was a long pause on the other end of the line. "I know you do. I blame myself. Because it was my fault."

"But worst of all, I hate that I idolized you and you didn't live up to it. I don't know how I can ever trust anyone or anything ever again. Especially because…in the end, I'm not any different than you. I'm two different men. I don't know how to reconcile that with anything."

There was nothing but the sound of broken breathing on the other end of the line. And when his father spoke, his voice was heavy.

"I failed you, Maximus, and nothing has ever brought me greater pain. Everything I did was for our family. For our betterment. And I'm responsible for the death of the woman you loved. I hate that. I hate how short my focus was. How arrogant I was about my own resilience. How I might've felt like I was untouchable, but didn't take into account the fact that my family was not. And that my family made me vulnerable. But... I'm not two different men. I am one. I'm very flawed. I care about the people in my life, but I can get blinded by my greed. By opportunity. I have a difficult time saying no. It's why I've engaged in business deals I should've walked away from. It's why I... That in the moment sometimes I forget my own principles. Because it's easier to say yes to what's right in front of me. Since Stella's death I've been better. But it doesn't take away what I did. It would be comforting to think that I was two men. But I'm just one broken one."

It was the strangest thing. That realization. Maximus remembered how he had felt in Annick's arms. Like he was one. The man and the beast. It had been comforting in a way. Even though in another it was easier to believe that one man was real and the other was a facade. Whichever felt better at the time.

Annick was the only one who knew. She saw him as one, and she claimed to love him anyway. She saw him. And she made him want to know what it would be like if he let go of everything that had happened in the past. Of the betrayal of his father, the loss of Stella and every black act he'd committed along the road to this point and accepted it. If he let go of the flaws in the world.

And knew the fact that he could never really quite balance the scales.

He had killed the man who had imprisoned Annick. Had removed him from power. Had set her free, but it didn't erase what had happened to her.

You could never erase the bad things in the past. You could only go forward. Otherwise… It was like Annick had said.

Seeing bars where there weren't any.

"How do you live with it? How do you live

with the flaws inside of you? How do you move forward?"

"I didn't have a choice. I love you. And Minerva and Violet. And I love your mother more than anything. And I have to live with myself. So there comes a point where you simply have to do just that. Live. Even if things don't seem fair. Even if the world is broken. Even if *you* are."

"I don't deserve her."

"I don't deserve your mother. I don't deserve the fact that you still speak to me, Maximus. I never have, and I don't take that for granted. I don't deserve Dante's loyalty, or Min and Violet's devotion. I can only accept your love. Because it's the only thing that makes living worth it. It's not the money. It's you."

It was the strangest thing. Because the world was still as it was, and his father had still made the mistakes he had. But there was a deep acceptance inside of him now that hadn't existed before. The world was broken and he couldn't fix it.

But he could love a woman who lived in this world. And she could love him. And with that love it was possible that they would make things better than he ever had with vengeance. Than he ever had with darkness.

There were no scales.

There was no cosmic scoresheet. There were tragedies. And there were triumphs. And there was right and wrong, and justice to be sure.

But mostly, there was love. And with love you could blot out a multitude of sins. If you were only brave enough to try.

"Thank you," Maximus said. "For helping me see." He hesitated for a moment. "I'm not who anyone in this family thinks I am."

"We should talk about it. Sometime. When you've settled things with your wife."

Maximus nodded. "All right. But I warn you that when you know the truth, you might not want me as a son anymore."

"Maximus, you have wanted me as a father in spite of my frailties. I could never not want you as a son."

Maximus hung up the phone and sat there for a long moment. Then the strongest, sharpest pain he'd ever felt pierced his chest. It was like dying. But he was still alive. Everything that he had tried not to feel since the attempt on Annick's life assaulted him then. It was no longer just anger. No longer a desperate need for revenge. He had nearly lost her. He had nearly lost her without ever truly having her. He had nearly lost her without ever telling her that he loved her. Without ever letting himself feel it. It was not protection. It was foolishness. It was fear.

And fear was a great liar.

He was gasping for breath now, barely able to.

He had told her he didn't love her. His Annick. He had hurt her. She had already been hurt so many times.

He did not deserve her. He didn't.

He doubled over with that knowledge. With that pain.

But she had said that she accepted him. All of him. Everything that he was.

Why? *How?*

He didn't have the answer.

But as he lay there, stunned by the full force of these emotions, he knew that it didn't matter why.

Because it wasn't fair.

Nothing about life was.

Not the childhood Annick had spent in the dungeon, the death of Stella or the fact that Annick loved him. Knowing all that he was.

None of it was fair.

It was better than fair.

It was love.

Annick was fed up with her own frailty at this point. She had lived through unimaginable cruelties, and she had not fallen apart. But that was the problem.She had not had the time then. Now she was safe, well taken care of and feeling quite ill-used. And she now had the luxury of reveling in it.

She missed Maximus. She missed everything about him. And she was ready to bind her own wrists and present herself in his bedchamber as a gift. For him to unwrap.

"Have a bit of pride," she said to herself.

She did not want pride. She wanted Maximus.

She lay across her bed, and as if her dreams had conjured him, there he suddenly was. Strong and silent and standing in the doorway, and she remembered what she had thought when she had seen him there in the dungeon. It was no longer bars, but him. He was not a prison, but a strange sort of freedom. A path to the center of herself. To all of her desires.

A man who was strong enough to take her anger, her grief, her joy, her pleasure.

A man who felt created most especially for her, but he did not seem to want to see it.

"What is this?" she asked, sitting up. "Are you here to brief me on military procedure?"

He shook his head. "No. I'm here to tell you... I'm not worthy of you. And I'm... I'm not two separate men. There's no monster in me. Just me. And it's been easier to pretend that I had a life in one place that was all its own, and a life in another that belonged to someone different. But it's all me. I took those missions because it was easier to do something than sit in grief. Because I was afraid of what I might do with my anger if I didn't channel it into something specific. I kept my old life because I still wanted to be near my family. Because I still loved my father even though I was angry with him. And

I never chose another person to love because I never even knew what love was.

"I was young and life was easy, and I fell into something good with a woman who was as light and happy as I was. And now I've seen dark things in the world. Atrocities. And knowing about all of that and having the strength to love anyway... Well, I wasn't strong enough to do that. Or brave enough. It took a woman who had seen as many terrible things as I had to make me want that again. Annick, from the moment I saw you it was something different. It was like you united both pieces of me. You made me have to figure out what it meant to be me. The Maximus King who cared about things. Who enjoyed pleasure. Who enjoyed life. And the Maximus King who was lost in a world of darkness and revenge. Wanting to protect you gave me purpose. And knowing you made me feel things again. Watching you live... I thought I was dead inside, but no. You made me into something so much better than I was even before."

"We are both broken, eh?"

"It's not being broken that defines us. It's love, don't you think?"

"Do you love me, Maximus?"

"Yes, Annick. I love you. Not like anyone ever before. Not like anything. I love you in a way I didn't think was possible."

"Maximus," she said, flinging herself up off the bed and wrapping her arms around his neck. Kissing him with everything she had inside of her.

"Thank you," he said. "For kidnapping me. I think you might've rescued me."

"Well, I know for certain that you rescued me. Maximus, whatever you want to call yourself, you are mine. Nothing else matters. I know what you've done." She spread her hands. "But you do not have blood on your hands. Many people were saved because of what you did. You had anger in your heart, yes. But you're a good man, and you always were. Your anger never took you to a place where you might harm an innocent. You were never a monster. Just wounded."

"Without all my mistakes, without all the pain, without all that I lost, I would never have made it to you. Whatever else I know to be true, I know that. You rescued me. You rescued me because of what you did. Set me free."

"And you set me free."

She had a strange, heavy sensation in her chest and looked toward the dresser. Her wedding bouquet was still there. She went over to it and grabbed hold of one of the flowers, breaking another blossom off. "For Stella," she said. "You would be proud of him. You would be proud of who he is. And I will take care of him. And love him."

"I hope you know," he said, putting his hand over hers, "that what I feel for you isn't the same. I loved her as a boy. I love you as a man."

Her heart lifted. "And I hope sometimes as a monster. Because I did quite like the monster."

"I will be whatever you wish. Your captor. Your protector. Your man. Your monster."

"You are all those things, I think. There is no pretending. Not with me."

"Never. And you don't need to pretend anymore either."

"No," she said. And she flung herself into

his arms, feeling every big thing she had done since he'd first come into her life. Hungry and happy and filled with a sharp, aching joy that made her vibrate. She wanted to lick him and fight him and kiss him all at once, and she would. She would.

"Me, I love you. And that is quite a brilliant thing."

He cupped her chin, his eyes touching her soul. "There are no bars, Annick, not now. All I see is you."

It was true—there were no words for the sort of pain she and Maximus had endured in their lives.

But there was love and joy that transcended language too. That could only be felt and breathed and lived. And they had that.

It made the world beautiful and magical, and bright enough to drown out all the darkness that had come before.

Always.

Forever.

EPILOGUE

MAXIMUS AND ANNICK built the most beautiful life out of the broken pieces they'd been given. It was not less. It was not secondary. It was everything. And when they welcomed their first child into the world, a boy, and Annick named him Marcus after her brother, Maximus felt joy like he'd never known before.

"You know," Annick said, looking at him as he held his son, "you were never dead inside, Maximus. You were just protecting yourself."

"Yes. To an extent. But I also didn't know. There was nothing in me that could ever have been prepared for the joy that was coming."

"Thank God for chloroform, eh?"

He chuckled, looking down at that tiny perfect life they had created, and all around at the beautiful, glittering life they had created in this world that was their own.

"Yes, Annick. Thank God for chloroform."

And for the small, determined woman who had believed in love, happy endings and kidnap, who had been strong enough and determined enough to redeem him and to save them both.

* * * * *

LET'S TALK
Romance

For exclusive extracts, competitions
and special offers, find us online:

f facebook.com/millsandboon

◎ @millsandboonuk

🐦 @millsandboon

Or get in touch on 0844 844 1351*

For all the latest titles coming soon,
visit millsandboon.co.uk/nextmonth

*Calls cost 7p per minute plus your phone company's price per
minute access charge

Want even more
ROMANCE?

Join our bookclub today!

'Mills & Boon books, the perfect way to escape for an hour or so.'

Miss W. Dyer

'Excellent service, promptly delivered and very good subscription choices.'

Miss A. Pearson

'You get fantastic special offers and the chance to get books before they hit the shops'

Mrs V. Hall

Visit millsandbook.co.uk/Bookclub and save on brand new books.

MILLS & BOON